WOLF'S HEAD

Fargo knew Lasher was behind attempts to wreck the MacKenzie logging operation. Lasher wanted the timberland for himself, and smashing MacKenzie was the first step. Fargo's old Rough Riders boss had an interest in the situation and wanted Lasher stopped — permanently. Lasher was as hard to catch as a greased pig, but when Fargo takes on an assignment he can handle it.

JOHN BENTEEN

WOLF'S HEAD

Complete and Unabridged

LINFORD
Leicester

First published in the
United States of America

First Linford Edition
published May 1994

British Library CIP Data

Benteen, John
  Wolf's head.—Large print ed.—
Linford western library
I. Title II. Series
823.914 [F]

ISBN 0–7089–7573–9

Published by
F. A. Thorpe (Publishing) Ltd.
Anstey, Leicestershire

Set by Words & Graphics Ltd.
Anstey, Leicestershire
Printed and bound in Great Britain by
T. J. Press (Padstow) Ltd., Padstow, Cornwall

This book is printed on acid-free paper

1

THE hotel on Seattle's Skid Road was about one cut above a flophouse. The room, with an iron bed and scabby linoleum on the floor, stank of its previous habitants: of dirt, sweat, stale smoke, bad whiskey. But Fargo did not intend to stay here long.

He was a big man, better than six feet, wide in the shoulders, narrow in the hips, his legs the long, lean tough ones of a horseman. His face was weathered, tanned, with high cheekbones and a rock of a jaw, the mouth a thin-lipped slash. Beneath white brows, his eyes were gray, cold, yet always alive, alert. He was still a few years away from forty, but his close-cropped hair was snow-white, prematurely so. He was ugly, no doubt about it, bearing the scars of many battles, but it was the kind of ugliness that made women look at him more than twice and come to him if he wanted them; a hard, thoroughly masculine ugliness.

Now, as easily as if it were empty, he hoisted the big trunk up on the sagging bed. Fishing a key from the watch-pocket of his canvas pants, he unlocked the heavy padlock and threw back the lid. For a moment, his eyes flared with pleasure as he looked down at its contents. They were the tools of his trade, which was fighting. He was a soldier of fortune, with long years of violent experience behind him. The violence had begun on a New Mexican ranch when his parents had been killed by raiding Apaches, who had somehow missed the only child. It had continued through a few years of servitude with foster parents on another ranch. At twelve, he'd had a bellyful of being an unpaid slave, kicked around by the miserly, sadistic foster father. He'd hauled out one night, on foot; never been back. Since then, he'd been on his own.

Punching cattle, hardrock mining, logging, he'd done it all. Growing into manhood as hard as hickory, he'd found his real profession in Bucky O'Neill's company of The Rough Riders in the Spanish-American War. He had everything it took to make a soldier, and he'd stayed on in the Cavalry through a hitch in the Philipines during the Insurrection when the fighting had been bitter between the Army and the natives who, freed of Spanish rule, were determined to be independent of America as well. That hard interval had made him a true professional. Since then, he had fought in little wars and revolutions all over the Western hemisphere, freelance. In between, he'd put in a stint as a boxer in the prize ring and once, really down on his luck, as bouncer in a New Orleans whorehouse. That was behind him now; he went where the money was, and he did not work cheap. There was no reason to; the rewards were good for a fighting man who knew his trade and had long since ceased to quibble over right and wrong.

Now, with respect, he unpacked the articles in the trunk. Weapons, good ones, tailor-made for his own purposes. He took out a Winchester .30-30 carbine in a fine leather saddle scabbard, extracted it, worked its lever once or twice, satisfied himself that it had survived the long train trip up from the border without damage. He laid it aside, fished from the trunk a pistol in a *buscadero* holster on a cartridge belt. It was an Officer's Model Colt .38 revolver, of the sort the Army had used before adopting the .45 automatic. The Army had said the .38 packed insufficient stopping power to halt the Moros of the Southern Philippines when they ran amok, full of hashish and fanaticism. Fargo had stopped lots of them with the .38; it was far more accurate and reliable than the .45; and the fact that he used hollow-pointed slugs that would explode on impact, doing terrible things to human flesh, made up for the difference in bullet-weight and powder-load.

He laid the Colt aside, took out a shoulder harness for it. That he put in another place; shortly, he would slip it on, transfer the pistol from the hip-holster to one that fitted under his left arm. Then, with a faint smile, like that of a man thinking of his lover, he took from the trunk the shotgun, in it's chamois-skin case.

It was disassembled; neatly he locked it together. A Fox Sterlingworth, ten-gauge, it had once been a long-barreled fowling piece. Fargo had cut the barrels off short, transforming it into a riot gun with open bores. He had added, too, the sling. Now he slung the sawed-off shotgun over his right shoulder so that it hung, muzzles-down, behind his back. He hooked his right thumb in the sling. Then he twitched that thumb, almost imperceptibly. With lightning speed the short barrels came up under his right arm, pointed forward, the gun upside down. In the same clocktick of time, Fargo's left hand lashed across his chest, hit both triggers at once. If the gun had been cocked and loaded, that incredibly fast motion would have hurled eighteen buckshot in a deadly spray toward his chosen target. At short range, it was the most lethal weapon man had yet devised; that spreading pattern of buckshot would chop up, mow down, anything in its path.

He was totally expert with it; and now he shifted it to the left shoulder and repeated the process. It was just as miraculously swift and would have been as deadly. He had been born with the ability to use either hand; being ambidextrous had saved his life more than once.

Fargo unslung the shotgun, but he did not put it aside at once. Instead, he looked down at its ornately chased, engraved, and inlaid receiver, reading the legend almost obscured amidst the fancy work: *To Neal Fargo. Gratefully, from T. Roosevelt*. His thumb traced the legend absently. It had been The Colonel who had put him on to this job.

The Colonel, Fargo remembered, had looked old, tired. After years of power — Police Commissioner of New York City, Governor of the State, Vice President and then President — power had been his meat and drink. Even without it, he still had to be on the go, and, naturalist and conservationist and generally feisty adventurer that he was, he had just returned from an exploration of the Amazon and its tributaries that had been full of hardship. That trip had taken its toll; still debilitated from fever, he had looked shrunken and sallow when he and Fargo had conferred secretly in El Paso, far from the robust figure he had cut as Colonel of The Rough Riders, when they had first come to know one another.

"You've worked in the woods," The

Colonel said. "Logging."

"Yes." Fargo rolled the drink of excellent bourbon between his palms. They were in The Colonel's hotel room, only the two of them, all the aides and understrappers banished.

"You know it well?"

"I'm a damned good timber beast," said Fargo without conceit.

"Then . . . " The Colonel hesitated, looking embarrassed. "You'd be ideal for the job. Except I can't pay you much."

Fargo looked back at him. This was the only living man whom he loved and respected. This was as close to a real father as he could remember. Between the two of them it had never been a matter of money; not since Fargo had saved The Colonel's life under fire in Cuba.

"If you got something you want me to do," he said, "I'll do it."

"I have. But it's hard to explain."

"Tell me anyhow."

"Yes." The Colonel had risen, had

8

begun to pace the room with that short, choppy stride of his. It lacked the old-time bounce. "Fargo," he said, "we're using up the country too fast."

"There's a lot of it," Fargo said.

"Not enough." The Colonel turned. "It seems like a lot now, yes, in 1916. But someday it won't be nearly enough. Someday this country will be full of people, big cities everywhere, all across it. Swarming with people."

"I hope I don't live to see that," said Fargo. "Before it gets like that, I'll hoist my tail and stampede out."

The Colonel looked almost sad. "I know. You and I — we're too much alike. We like the lonesome places; when we see smoke from other people's fires, it bothers us. You're not cut out for civilization and neither am I really. But that doesn't change things. People go on breeding, immigrants keep on coming, we're going to fill up. When that happens, if we're not careful, we'll rape this country. Gouge out all its minerals, cut down all its trees, turn it into a desert." His lips thinned beneath his gray mustache. "It's happened before. Civilizations — mighty ones — have fallen because they laid waste the land. Look at Greece, barren now. Look at North Africa — desert where once there was fertility. You've seen it in your time, here in Texas. Overgrazing, the land grown up in cactus and chapparal where once it was horse-high in good grass. The big game killed off. Farmers coming in and plowing up ground that's going to blow away sooner or later because there's not enough rainfall to keep it from turning to dust."

"I've seen that," Fargo said. "It makes me sick. That's why I spend more time south of the border these days."

"All right," The Colonel said. "Wood, timber. God knows, we seem to have plenty of it now. But we don't really. You know, there are two ways of logging — selective cutting and what the loggers call highball, cut-and-get-out. Meaning, chop down everything in sight, turn the land to wasteland, and the hell with anything except profit."

"That's the way most of them operate."

"Right. And it's a crime. Selective cutting is what they ought to be doing. Conservation — " He chopped the air with a hand. "When I was President, I made it one of the key-notes of my administration. We set up national parks and forests, restocked big game, tried to preserve something of this country for generations to follow. But now I'm out of power, and things are different."

"How?" asked Fargo.

The Colonel sat down, picked up his drink. "You ever hear of the Wolf's Head Tract?"

"The Wolf's Head," Fargo said, after a moment. "Yeah. Virgin timber, Douglas fir, up the Wolf's Head River. Government owns it all, has, ever since

11

they signed a treaty with the Indians years ago."

"Right." The Colonel's eyes glittered. "When I was President, we set that aside as a preserve. But the lumbermen want that timber. All right, timber's necessary; the country needs wood. But there's a right way to go at it and a wrong one. If it's cut properly, selective cutting, taking out only the marketable trees and leaving the rest to reseed, raise another crop of fir, the Wolf's Head will be an invaluable national resource for generations."

"I see," Fargo said.

"The lumber interests in Congress were finally successful in forcing Interior to put logging rights to the Wolf's Head out for bids. The specifications were strict: selective logging, in accordance with best practice. Cutting so something will be left for the future. Whoever bid had to agree to that."

"So what's the problem?"

"Great Northwestern, run by Alec MacKenzie, was the successful bidder.

Alec and I have hunted together; he's a good man, Fargo, an honest one. He stuck his neck out a mile to bid in these timber rights. He's following the letter of the law, observing the terms of the contract down to every crossed T and dotted I. It's costing him money, the kind of money the cut-and-get-out logger would never spend. But that's the way Alec is."

The Colonel took a long swallow of his drink. "He stretched himself thin, mighty thin, Fargo, to bid in the Wolf's Head Tract. He's got to make a payment to Interior come winter when his drive's gone down the river and been paid for at the mills. If he doesn't, he's in default and the contract, the logging rights, go to Lasher Lumber Company, the next high bidder."

Fargo's eyes narrowed. "Saul Lasher?"

"You know him?"

"He's a sonofabitch," said Fargo. "He'd cut his own grandmother's throat for a nickel. They ran him out of northern Michigan on account of the way he operated. When he gets through cutting, there's nothing left behind him — nothing."

"Exactly," said The Colonel. "If MacKenzie doesn't meet his payments, Lasher gets the Wolf's Head Tract by default. And Lasher will turn the whole country into a desert. A hundred years from now, it'll still be desert." He stared at Fargo. "I don't want MacKenzie to default. I don't want Lasher to get his hands on the Wolf's Head."

"Is that where I come in?"

"That's where you come in. Alec MacKenzie's having a devil of a time. Sabotage . . . Everything is going wrong. Probably Lasher's hired men inside MacKenzie's outfit to screw him up, but Alec can't put his hand on them. Anyhow, he's way behind schedule in his cutting. If he doesn't cut more timber, make his drive successfully down the Wolf's Head to Puget Sound, he's finished and Lasher gets the lease. I don't want to see

14

that happen. The country can't afford to have that happen." The Colonel paused. "You're an expert logger. You also happen to be the finest fighting man I know. Fargo, you've got to see that MacKenzie comes through, gets the timber out, makes his drive down the river, is able to pay the Government. It's not just a matter of dollars and cents for a friend of mine, it's a matter of the country's welfare."

Fargo stood up, uncoiling his tall length like a lazy snake. "I ain't been in the woods for a long time. Maybe it'll be a nice change."

"Wait a minute," The Colonel said. "I told you, I couldn't pay you much."

"The hell with what you can pay," Fargo said. "How much profit will MacKenzie make if he don't lose this lease?"

The Colonel frowned. "At least a quarter of a million. Maybe more."

Fargo smiled. He took out a long, thin, black cheroot, clamped it between perfect white teeth, and struck a match. Through smoke, he looked at the man across the table.

"It ought to be worth ten per cent of that to MacKenzie to get his logs out on time," he said.

The Colonel stared back, then gave a short, barking laugh. "Yes. Yes, by Jove, I dare say it would be."

"So you don't have to pay me anything," Fargo said. "I can strike a deal with him."

"Yes," said The Colonel. "Yes, certainly. But, Fargo — "

"Uh-huh."

"I should warn you. When MacKenzie got in touch with me, he told me that he had already put three undercover agents in his camps to see who was trying to break him. All three died. There are accidents in logging camps. One was killed by a choker cable when it broke and lashed. Another was crushed under a falling tree. A third was found drowned in a creek near one of their cutting areas."

Fargo's lips curled. "Were they professionals?"

"Loggers? Yes."

"I mean fighting men."

For a moment the man across from him was silent. Then he said, "Not like you."

Fargo's grin widened. He rolled the cigar across his mouth. "All right," he said.

The Colonel smiled. "You'll try it?"

"Sure," said Fargo. "I'll catch the night train north."

* * *

Now he reluctantly laid the shotgun aside. Then, from the trunk he took a knife. It was a weapon of strange design with a ten-inch blade in a specially-molded sheath. Hinged handles of water buffalo horn folded down over six inches of that shaft of hardened steel which could be driven through a silver dollar with a single blow without blunting or dulling. It came

17

from Southern Luzon, was called a Batangas knife, and Fargo was as much expert with it as with his guns. He hefted it now in his right hand, with the handles closed around the blades; then he flipped the handle catch and his hand jerked and suddenly the whole ten inches of glittering blade was naked and ready for lethal use. He smiled, flicked his hand again, and the blades closed up. Then he sheathed the knife. Later, when he went to the woods, it would ride in his hip pocket.

Next, from within the trunk, he took out the bandoliers. They were designed to criss-cross his chest, one holding fifty rounds of shotgun ammunition, the other studded with rifle cartridges. In the bottom of the trunk was a supply of extra ammunition for all his firearms; he was careful about his cartridges. One bad round could cost his life in this business; and he either loaded them himself or bought them only from people he could trust.

Beneath the guns and ammo were his

clothes. They fit every occasion, from riding hard in Mexico with Villa against the Government, to sledging across Alaska where he had, on occasion, finding mining too tedious, dealt faro and played poker, using his skill as a professional gambler to relieve the suckers, who really worked the creeks, of their accumulated dust. What he chose now, however, were canvas pants — stagged short, their bottoms cut off — and heavy leather boots with sharp steel caulks. Logger's boots.

He stripped off his regular trousers, climbed into the stagged pants, threw aside the leather cavalry officer's boots he usually wore and laced on the logger's footgear. Then, arising, he slid the Colt into the shoulder harness, buckled it around his torso, and donned a light jacket — Seattle was chilly, even in late summer — to conceal it. He slid the Batangas knife on his belt, sheathed it in his hip pocket. Then he put everything else back into the trunk, locked it, and slid it beneath the bed.

He lighted a cigar and, with it clamped between his teeth, picked up his hat. It was a cavalry soldier's hat, weathered, stained, broadbrimmed, and he set it on his head at a jaunty angle. Then he went downstairs. The iron caulks of his boots tore splinters from the stair treads, but they had already been chopped to pieces by the boots of many timber beasts in years gone by. Then he went out onto Skid Road.

In other towns, the name had been corrupted to Skid Row. But in a timber town like Seattle or Tacoma or Portland, Skid Road meant not a final resting place for bums but the endless rows of honky-tonks and dead-falls where the loggers had their blasts when they came to civilization again out of the lonely woods. After months in the woods, they wanted whiskey, bright lights, gambling and, above all, women. Skid Road undertook to provide their needs.

Fargo strolled past doors spilling light into darkness, pouring out the tinny sounds of ragtime music. MacKenzie had told him where to go; Big Duke Hotchkiss would be in a place called The Blue Ox. And Hotchkiss was the woods boss, the superintendent, the man he had to see.

Fargo had caught MacKenzie at the office on the wharf near the sound where boomed rafts of logs floated in still water before entering the mill, their butt ends branded with Great Northwestern's GN mark. In the privacy of MacKenzie's office he had showed the man the letter from The Colonel.

MacKenzie had been a typical Scot, tall, stringy, dour, and with honesty like steel shining through the sour surface. He handed back the letter, said, "So you're the one."

"Right," said Fargo.

"It's a dangerous job ye're undertaking," MacKenzie gnawed his pipe. "All my other men have been dealt with harshly. But someone in the Wolf's Head operation is working against me.

21

If I don't find out who it is, I'm in bad trouble."

"And if you do," Fargo said, "and he's balked, then you're a quarter of a million ahead."

MacKenzie's cold blue eyes flickered. "Aye," he said, finally.

"I want twenty thousand if I succeed. If your drive makes it to Puget Sound and you meet your lease payment."

"Mon, that's a mort of money."

"Not near as much as if you lose your whole investment."

"True." The Scot took the pipe from between yellowed teeth. "And if you fail?"

"If I fail, they'll bury me out on the Wolf's Head Tract. You pay for results, not promises."

He was talking MacKenzie's language. A smile broke through the glacial facade. "Mon, ye're on. Shake on it." He put out his hand, and Fargo knew instinctively that the grasp of it was as good as a written contract.

"But," MacKenzie said, "I can't send

ye out to the camp myself. Ye've got to clear through Big Duke."

"Hotchkiss? I've heard of him. Top bull of the woods in any man's language."

"Aye, but mean and hard. He does all the hiring, and he's persnickety about it. It would excite suspicion if I went over his head. You've got to con him into taking you on."

Fargo nodded. "I'll do that, one way or the other. Tell me, you got any leads at all? Who's slowing down your operation?"

"Not Hotchkiss, if that's what ye're thinkin'. The Duke and I have worked together twenty years. He's wholly loyal. But — " MacKenzie gestured. "We're high-lead loggers, ye're familiar with that?"

Fargo nodded. "Sure. Mechanized."

"Aye. Nowadays, it's the only economical way. But when ye use machinery, ye're at the mercy of machinery. A boiler blows out on a donkey engine, ye're out of action.

23

A bull-block breaks on a spar tree, another day lost, maybe more if ye've no spare block in camp. Somebody files a choker collar line in two, it breaks, cuts a man in half with its whiplashin' and yet, ye've no concrete proof. Boilers blow, blocks freeze up, cables snap . . . And it all adds up, a day here, a day there, until you're weeks behind your schedule. Still, Duke's not mixed up in it, on that I'll risk me own life. We've known each other too long. Despite all obstacles, he gets out the sticks of timber. Come fall when the Wolf's Head runs full, we'll drive those down to the Sound and then to the mill. Can you ride a log, use a peavey or a cant-hook?"

"I've run a lot of rivers in my time," said Fargo.

"That's where the crucial moment'll come. If we get the fir out of the woods and into the river, there's no way anybody can stop us then but to block the drive." MacKenzie's eyes had narrowed. "Still, a log drive's the most dangerous ride known to man. Been many a year since I've bounced a stick of timber down the river meself, but God knows how many good friends I've seen ground up between the logs when they lost their balance and fell, not to mention those lucky ones that just drowned. When the big log drive starts, nothing can stop it save a jam; if a man falls in the way, tough luck."

Fargo had arisen. "You don't have to tell me about a drive; I've ridden my share. Where will I find Hotchkiss?"

"At The Blue Ox. Be subtle with him, Fargo. Make him hire ye as an ordinary hand."

"I'll do my best," Fargo said, and he had gone out.

Now, confronting the doors of The Blue Ox, he hesitated. Then he slammed them open, went in noisily, drawing attention to himself. He had thought about it now, and he knew what role he would play unless somebody recognized him and fouled him up. There was one sure way to get hired by a man like Hotchkiss . . .

Inside, he scanned the bar room through swirling smoke. It seethed with loggers in from the woods after the latest drive. They were trying to soak up as many memories as they could before they went out in the brutal environment of a logging camp. For them, memories consisted of monumental drunks about which they could later brag and as many women as they could buy before their money ran out.

The Blue Ox was doing its best to provide plenty of both. Waiters scurried back and forth with trays, and women were everywhere, hardfaced harpies wearing next to nothing, legs and breasts revealed by scanty costumes designed to arouse lonely men and con them into buying drinks. Fargo, for the moment, was not interested in the women. He was looking for Duke Hotchkiss.

Then he picked him out, a giant, a monumental figure in the drift of swirling smoke. He had a woman on each side, his massive arms wrapped around both of them, his big hands playing over their nearly naked breasts. Fargo grinned faintly. Then he went on down the bar. He came up behind the tall man, a good four inches above his own height. He slammed him on the back. "Hey, Duke!"

Hotchkiss turned, blinking pale blue eyes in a face burned dark by years in the woods. He was about Fargo's age, all muscle, an absolute bull in plaid shirt and stagged pants and caulked boots. He stared at Fargo, "Who the hell are you?" he asked thickly.

"Neal Fargo. Hear you're hiring for the fall cut, want a job."

Hotchkiss's wide mouth twisted. Fargo liked that open, honest, almost handsome face. It was a shame, what he might have to do to it. "Go away, goddammit," Hotchkiss snapped. His hands tightened on the breasts of the two girls. "Can't you see I'm busy?"

"I want a job," said Fargo doggedly.

"A job as what? I got a full ticket, I

don't need no men! Now, will you hit the road? Go see Lasher, maybe he's hirin'!" Hotchkiss turned away.

Fargo smiled, thin lips twisting in his weathered face. When it came, this was going to be a fight worth remembering. He had not had such a fight in a long time. Maybe he would not even win it. Duke Hotchkiss was a hell of an opponent. But, either way, it would be worth remembering. He grabbed Hotchkiss by the shoulder. "Hey, Duke . . . "

The big man whirled. Now his face was angry. "Look, feller, I told you, my ticket's full, I don't need nobody. Go peddle your goddamn papers."

"Don't talk to me like that," said Fargo. "Listen, I can do anything in the woods you need. I can fall or buck or run the donkey, rig or climb and ride the drive. I got to have a job, and you got to take me on."

Again those pale eyes blinked. Then Hotchkiss smiled faintly. "Buddy," he said, "I don't got to do a goddamn thing except maybe cave your face in."

That was what Fargo was waiting for. He backed away.

"I got to fight you to hire on?" he asked softly.

"You fight me, you won't be in no shape to hire on."

"Suppose I whip you," Fargo said.

Hotchkiss stared, then laughed. "Nobody ain't never whipped me yet. You do it, you can have any job on the ticket, even if I got to bump somebody off."

Fargo raised his clenched fists, spat on his knuckles. "That's what I got to do to earn some wages," he said, smiling, "then come on."

Hotchkiss stood straight, towering over him, looking at him incredulously. "Why, you pimplehead — " Then he laughed. "Okay. You wanta die, then it's your affair." He raised huge, clubbed hands and charged.

2

ARGO weaved instinctively, like a shadow. He heard a fist go by his ear with an express-train sh. He did not even try to return he blow, but brought up, instead a booted foot. It's spiked sole caught Duke Hotchkiss in mid-charge and the man bellowed. That painful impact would have been enough to drop an ordinary human, but Duke only reeled back, slightly dazed. In that instant, Fargo came in.

He slipped between the man's guard, sickened as Duke was with that low blow. His right fist slammed against something like a granite wall and snapped Duke's head back with the force of a mule's kick. His knuckles burned with the impact. But with his left, he drove into a web of muscle only a little less unresilient than a tree trunk — Hotchkiss's belly.

Duke whoofed, eyes bulging, back slamming against the bar. The woods boss spread wide arms, sucked in a long breath, lost it as Fargo hit him again in the gut. But then, measuring his opponent, finding himself at last confronted by a professional fighting man, he let out a grunt of joy. Fargo recognized the sound; here, Duke was saying, was a foe worthy of his steel. Fargo charged again, wanting to deal out all possible punishment, but now Duke, exhilarated, was ready for him. Fargo ran into a pile driver.

Actually, it was a sluggish fist moving in past his guard. It caught him on the jaw and the world blanked out until he slammed against the room's far wall. He brought up hard, the high-pitched shrieking of the whores and bar girls in his ears. He blinked dazed eyes; then something blotted out all light: the huge form of Duke Hotchkiss boring in.

Instinctively, Fargo raised his boot,

but Duke dodged the caulked sole. Then Duke hit him with a looping left that picked Fargo up and sent him hurtling through the air. He landed on a table, its legs smashed and buckled under the impact, and Duke changed direction, was diving after him. Fargo reached out, seized a broken table leg, brought it up, and Duke's chin slammed against its shattered stub. The big man sighed and went rolling off. Fargo came out of the wreckage of the table and was on him like a panther. He would have finished Duke then, but the big man got a knee up. Like a cocked trigger, it folded under Fargo, then snapped out. Its tremendous strength sent Fargo sailing backwards, and he slammed into the bar. For an instant, he thought his back was broken, but there was no time to feel sorry for himself, Duke was up and coming, charging.

Fargo did a back flip. He went over the bar like a tumbler, landing hard behind it, crouching. Duke's launching drive sent him sliding across the mahogany top and, like a rocket, he kept on going, big head slamming through bottles on the back-bar, sending them flying. The mirror smashed, broken glass falling all around, as Duke's head chunked against it. Simultaneously, Fargo, from below, kicked Hotchkiss in the belly.

But he might as well have tried to stop a landslide. Duke growled, fell, landed fair on Fargo behind the bar. Fargo's outstretched hand found a bottle; he brought it down clubbed, smashed it over Hotchkiss's lank, black-haired crest. Whiskey and blood mingled, but Duke only laughed as a big hand went out and found Fargo's throat and two hundred and forty pounds of hard muscle bound Fargo to the floor, as his other hand caught Fargo's wrist and blocked the onslaught of the broken bottle. It crunched bone, and Fargo dropped the bottle. The Duke, laughing with sheer pleasure, was choking Fargo to death.

But he'd left Fargo too much leeway. Fargo brought up a booted foot. It caught, with contortion, the back of Hotchkiss's skull. Duke's eyes bulged; for a second, his hand relaxed its clasp. That was all Fargo needed, his own hand came up, splayed across Duke's face and, in that instant, Fargo bucked.

Duke went flying backwards. Fargo laughed now and came up as if he were made of rubber. He threw himself forward in a dive, evading Duke's reflexive knee, landed hard on the woods boss's sprawled frame. Straddling it, he hit Duke's granite jaw again and again and again.

But the man was indestructible. Duke surged up like a dog shaking off water, and Fargo was dislodged. He fell backward, bounded up again. As Duke charged him, he vaulted over the bar. Duke hurtled past, brought up short, turned. Fargo backed away into the room. Duke leaped the bar and came for him.

Fargo seized a chair, raised it high, and brought it down. It smashed over Duke's head and shoulders but it might as well have been so many matchsticks. Duke kept coming. Fargo kicked a table in his way; Duke booted it aside. Now Fargo was against the wall again. He ducked as Duke lashed out, and the whole room shook when Duke's fist slammed against the plaster. Fargo came up from down low, caught that granite chin from underneath. It was a blow like the explosion of a stick of dynamite. Duke rocked back. Fargo came again, hit him in the belly. Duke, even falling, lobbed a sideways blow that caught Fargo alongside the head, sending him sprawling.

Then they were apart, both on the floor. Heads reeling, they scrambled unsteadily to their feet. Now they knew they were evenly matched Hotchkiss had an edge of size and strength, Fargo of knowledge and footwork. It all cancelled out. They loped toward each other, breathing raspingly. Both were bleeding, bruised and swollen. Still, neither would give up. The room was silent, patrons of the bar making around them a wide and liberal circle.

Fargo had not been whipped in years. Still, in his time he had been beaten and knew what it felt like. He was very close to being beaten now. But he was never beaten until he could fight no more, not even raise a fist. He was the first to charge.

When he went in, he ducked instinctively and Duke's windmilling counterblow whizzed overhead. Fargo struck high up in the belly for the solar plexus, and felt his fist connect with that spot of vulnerability. Duke sighed and sat down on a table. Fargo aimed a blow at his head, but the table broke and he missed as Duke dropped beneath the roundhouse swing.

The Duke grabbed one of Fargo's booted feet, big hands closing around the ankle. He upended it and Fargo went down hard. Duke arose, still holding the foot. "Goddamn," he husked and went plunging toward the door, spraying blood from his nose, dragging Fargo like a sack of meal.

Fargo bumped across the threshhold, over the sidewalk, into the oiled dirt street. His head rang, but he was helpless. Duke released him. "Now, you sonofabitch," Duke grated, and he raised high a boot studded with sharp caulks, designed to give a logger purchase in spruce or fir wood. Each caulk was like a little dagger, and when that boot slammed home, Fargo would be dead, his head pulped. The boot came down.

He rolled, caught the ripping caulks on his shoulder, seized Duke's foot, twisted it, and sent Duke sprawling. Duke hurtled out into the center of the street, plowing up gravel with his chin. Fargo scrambled up, gasping. He had no breath, no strength left; either this had to be finished now or he was done. He ran toward Duke.

Duke tried to rise. Fargo kicked him in the flank. Duke made a moaning sound, rolled away. Fargo pursued him. Duke came up, reached his knees. Fargo kicked with all the strength in his left leg. The steel toe of his logger's boot came up and caught Duke beneath the chin. The kick's force straightened out all the great heavy length of the woods boss's body and sent it flying. It landed hard in the center of the street. Fargo kept after it. When it landed he straddled it, seized Duke's black greasy hair in his left hand, yanked up his head, and slammed blow after blow against that rock-like chin with his right.

Beneath him, Duke sighed, relaxed, out cold.

Fargo, panting, let the man's head drop. He sat astride Duke for a second longer, lungs heaving like bellows. The whole fight had not lasted five minutes; to Fargo, it had seemed an hour, a lifetime. He barely had strength to get to his feet, and when he made it, he stood there shivering as if with chill, blood running from nose, mouth, and ears. But, strangely, he was grinning.

It had been, he thought, a lovely fight.

Then the crowd surged around him. Hands plucked at him. "Jesus, feller, you done cold-cocked Duke!" "Hell, man, nobody ever whupped ole Duke before!" "Buddy, you better clear out before Duke wakes up!" They chattered all around him, loggers and their women.

Fargo licked his broken lips. "Bring a bucket, somebody."

"Got one here, fulla water," It was thrust into his hands, which bled from every knuckle.

"Good." With the remnant of his strength, he upended the wooden piggin, dumped cold Sound water on Duke's head.

The big man snorted, rolled his head, opened his eyes. He stared up at Fargo, tried to rise. Fargo put a foot in the center of his chest, bore him downward. "Easy, Duke."

"Damn — " Duke batted swollen lids over puffy, bleeding eyes. But he sank back beneath Fargo's boot.

"Now," said Fargo. "You wanta go around again, we'll both take a breather first."

Duke's head rolled in negation. "Go around again? Jest as soon have a redwood drop on me . . . Christ, man. You've whipped me."

"Just barely," Fargo said. Then his legs gave out, and he dropped down to sit beside Duke in the dust. "Do I get the job?"

With bloody, shaking hands, Duke took out a smashed pack of cigarettes. From it, he extracted two crumpled smokes, passed one to Fargo, who lipped it gratefully. His own hand trembled as he struck a match, held it for Hotchkiss. The Duke inhaled, blew a plume of smoke.

"Buddy," he said, "if you kin use a double-bit ax and a crosscut like you can use them fists, you and me together can cut over the Wolf's Head all by ourselves. Whoever the hell you are, you're on."

"My name is Fargo. Neal Fargo."

Hotchkiss stared. "Fargo? *That* Fargo? The one that broke the jam at the Salmon Rapids back in 1912?"

"That one."

Hotchkiss let out a shuddering breath. "You oughta told me."

"Then we'd have missed a good fight."

The Duke laughed, a deep, joyful sound. "By God, wouldn't we?" He and Fargo lurched unsteadily to their feet. Then Hotchkiss's big hand slammed Fargo between the shoulder blades. "Okay! When somebody whips the Duke, the Duke buys! Let's go, Fargo! The drinks are on me!"

In the back room of The Blue Ox, Fargo and Hotchkiss killed a bottle. And Duke drew for him a picture far clearer and more forbidding than either The Colonel or MacKenzie had.

"There's lotsa fine timber on the

Wolf's Head, Fargo, you never seen no prettier fir. But damn it, she's a bitch to log; I never seen no harder chance. All straight up and down, and Judas! You got to fight for ever' stick of timber you git out." He sighed. "All the easy loggin's gone. I can remember when you could cut right on the hills above the Sound, just give the logs a push and they was in the water, boomed, and ready to tow. Now you got to go so far back in the mountains they got to pipe the sunlight in before you can find a tree taller than your armpit."

He drank, long and deep. "It wouldn't be so bad, neither, if we could jest cut where we wanted to when we pleased. But The Old Man's lease says we cut a certain way and that's how we cut and no other. And we got a deadline to meet — a time contract with the mills. We got to deliver so many board feet and we got to have the logs there by such and such a time, and if we don't, that contract goes to Lasher and then The Old Man'll default on his lease payment and Lasher'll get the Wolf's Head, too, and Great Northwestern's finished. And the hell of it is, it's a jinxed job." He shook his head. "Ever'thing that can go wrong has gone wrong. I always figgered I was a pretty good woods boss, but I've never tackled a cut like this. I've lost more men on this job — killed — than in all the other chances I ever bossed, and got less timber to show for it. It's jinxed, okay. I guess that's what comes from havin' a woman in camp."

Fargo sat up straight. "Woman?"

"Girl. Damm pretty, too — a real doll baby. Only she's off limits, so don't git all hot. Name's Barbara Mannix, her daddy's the Government timber cruiser on the job, stationed with us permanently to check our cutting, see that we stick to the contract terms. You know and I know, Fargo, a woman's got no more business in a loggin' camp than I'd have in a

Ladies' Aid Society. I got to admit, she keeps clear of the timber beasts, don't cause no trouble, but I still say, a woman in camp's a Jonah and no two ways about it!"

Fargo nodded thoughtfully. "Sounds like a mean deal all the way around."

"Be even meaner when we finally drive to the mill. That Wolf's Head River is tough as hell, especially in the fall floods. You know this country, it's always rainin', but we really git it come November, two or three months from now. That's when the Wolf's Head runs full, and that's when we take our sticks down to the Sound."

"No other way to get the timber out?"

"None. That country's so rough you can't build roads or rail lines through it even if the Government would let you. And it won't. So we dam the Wolf's Head, build our booms of logs up there and when the floods come, we blow the dam and down we go. The way the Wolf's Head falls down those mountains it's gonna be a real roller-coaster ride. What makes it bad is nobody's ever driven that river before. But I've been down it in a boat and there's chutes and gorges and whirlpools and falls in there that are like nothin' you ever imagined." He drank again. "Anyhow, that's the layout. Might as well stock up on booze now. None allowed in camp, and it's gonna be a long, dry summer."

★ ★ ★

It was well after midnight when Fargo left The Blue Ox, head buzzing with whiskey and the fight's after-effects, his body aching in every joint and muscle. Seattle's night life, however, was still going strong; drunken men and raucous women prowled the streets; hard-eyed girls stood in doorways, beckoning; bums snored in alleys or hung around street corners, panhandling the free-spending loggers.

45

Two blocks toward the hotel from The Blue Ox, one of these bums blocked Fargo's way — a bent, shuffling figure in heavy, tattered overcoat, toboggan cap pulled down almost over his face, although the night was not nearly that chilly. Fargo tried to dodge him, but the man stepped sideways, would not let him by. His left hand was held out, big and grimy; his right thrust deep in the pocket of the overcoat. "Feller, I ain't et in two days — "

"All right," said Fargo with resignation. He dug in his pants for change. In that instant, the panhandler moved closer.

"Don't twitch, don't yell," his voice rasped. "I got a Banker's Special in my pocket, and she's pointed right at your gut."

Fargo froze, cursing himself for being off-guard. Too much booze, and the battering Duke had dealt him. "You'll never get away with a stick-up here."

"Don't let it bother you," the man said sardonically. He backed away, and Fargo saw the muzzle of the gun against the cloth, knew he had told the truth. Knew, too, from the way that he slipped out of reach of any sudden play that he was no amateur; he was a professional. Then the fellow said, "You keep your hands out and clear. One funny move and you're gone." He jerked his head toward an alley a few feet away. "In there, nice and quiet and easy."

There was nothing for it but to obey. Normally, perhaps, Fargo could have overcome even such a dead drop, but he was heavy with fatigue, his reflexes slow, his hands swollen and stiff from the fight with Hotchkiss. No chance, yet. Still, in that clocktick, he became totally sober, totally alert.

He turned, entered the alley. The man came behind him. "Now, elevate those hands all the way and keep moving."

Fargo obeyed. They traveled the length of the alley which was lit just faintly enough from second-story windows overhead to eliminate any chance that Fargo might make a break in darkness. As he walked, hands lifted obediently, he asked, "Who sent you — Lasher?"

"Shut up."

But, he thought, it had to be. Saul Lasher was a bastard, but a smart one. He must have been keeping MacKenzie's office under surveillance, maybe even had a spy planted there. Fargo's conference with MacKenzie had not gone unnoticed. And somebody had recognized Fargo, knew his trade now — trouble-shooter for hire. Somebody who didn't want him to make it to the camp at the Wolf's Head Tract. Lasher was the only one.

They reached the alley's end. It gave on to a narrow, darkened street. Now the waterfront was not far; its pungent brackish smell freighted the wind. "Turn left," said the gunman from behind Fargo. He obeyed. They moved toward the docks. Now he could see lights across the harbor shimmering on the water, the log booms floating outside the mills, the dark shapes of tugs and towboats. They reached an old, splintered wharf, totally deserted. A rotten scow, abandoned, floated at anchor below its pilings. "Right up to the edge," the gunman said.

Fargo bit his lip. When he reached the edge, a single shot and down he'd go into the water. Neatly disposed of. But he kept moving, acutely aware of the gun trained on his back. Foot by foot, step by step, he approached the wharf's end. Another two strides, three, and then it would come. He had to do something and do it fast. But the minute his upraised hand moved, his captor would pull the trigger. And not even he was fast enough to dodge a bullet at point-blank range.

Now he reached the water's edge. "All right," the man said and, in that instant, Fargo fell forward. The gun roared; he heard the whine of lead over his head as he toppled off the dock's end. He hit the water headfirst, went under, clawing at the shoulder-holstered .38 even as it closed over his head.

He went down, kicked backwards, came up beneath the wharf. The water was foul, icy; he was racked with shudders. He shook his head, clearing eyes and nose, sucked up a gulp of air, seized a rotten crossbrace, sank low, sheltered by the wharf, his nearly submerged head a tiny target.

Above, he heard the scuffle of footsteps on the dock. "Goddamn" the gunman rasped. Fargo grinned; then, the Colt in hand, he ducked, dropped beneath the surface. His heavy boots and jacket weighed him down but he didn't have far to swim. He kicked under the hulk of the scow alongside the dock. It was an abandoned wanigan, maybe ten feet wide, twenty long, the boat in which the bedrolls and supplies for a river drive were carried. He pushed beneath its keelless hull, broke water in the shelter of its gunwale on the side away from the wharf. He hoisted up, caught the gunwale with his left hand, pulled his body half out of the water. Now he could see the dock. Snub-nosed gun out and raised, the man in the overcoat was a dark blot, bent over the end, staring at the place where Fargo had vanished.

Fargo's lips twisted in a smile like a wolf's snarl. He wanted a full, front-on shot. He spat foul water. Then he yelled, "Over here!"

Instinctively, the man jumped up, whirled. He threw the gun down into line; he must have had cat's eyes to spot Fargo's head so quickly. But Fargo had already aimed. Now he pulled the trigger.

The hollowpoint smashed the gunman right beneath the breastbone. It's explosive impact sent tatters of overcoat flying, as its impetus picked up the man and threw him over the wharf's side. Fargo heard the splash when he hit. There had been no outcry, and only the single shot.

Fargo laughed soundlessly. Then he

allowed his teeth to chatter as he pulled himself up aboard the old wanigan, from thence to the wharf by rusted ladder spikes set into a piling. Cautiously he made the wharf's deck, head swiveling, eyes straining to pierce the darkness. This area of warehouses and deserted buildings was empty of all life; the assassin had picked a good, safe spot for a killing. He went to the edge, looked over. There was no sign of the body. That overcoat would drag it down. Much later, when it had swollen with the gases of death, it would, perhaps surface. By then, he'd be bound for the Wolf's Head. Meanwhile, he thought, grinning, Lasher could wonder what had become of his hired hand.

He turned away. When he did, his foot kicked something that skittered across the wharf. He traced it down, picked it up — the gunman's snub-nosed pistol. He checked it, made sure it was fully loaded. Holstering his own Colt beneath his jacket, he slipped the short gun into his jacket pocket. All the way back to the hotel — to all appearances a drunk who'd fallen into the Sound and managed to get out — he kept his hand on it, ready in case there was another attempt. Next time, he'd not be caught napping.

But there was no next time. He made the hotel safely, ignoring the pimply-faced kid who served as night clerk and who stared at him as he dripped through the tiny lobby. In his room he locked the door. Switching on the light, he peeled off his sodden clothes, rubbed himself down with a towel from the wash stand. Teeth still chattering, he went to a bottle on the battered dresser, pulled the cork with strong, white teeth, and drank long and deeply. That stopped the shivering.

He pulled clean longjohns over the hard, muscular torso scarred with ancient wounds, the long lean legs that also bore their share of souvenirs of a rough and dangerous life. He double-checked the door lock and the window.

Then he went to bed. But not before he laid the double-barreled sawed-off Fox beside him like a mistress where he could snatch it up in case Lasher tried again.

3

HE had one more day in Seattle before Duke Hotchkiss and the crew pulled out for the Wolf's Head. When he awakened the next morning, most of the effects of the night before were gone; his finely tuned body had absorbed them while he slept. He dressed in fresh clothes, not logger's gear, but shirt, tie, corduroy jacket, whipcord pants and his cavalry boots. As always, he clamped the cavalry hat, retrieved from the wharf where it had fallen, on his head at a jaunty angle. With the shoulder-holstered Colt in place and his hand on the snub-nosed pistol taken from the gunman in his pocket, he went out, found a restaurant that looked decent, engulfed a huge breakfast of steak, eggs, flapjacks.

That hunger satisfied, he began to feel another. It had been a long time since he'd had a woman. Once he pulled out for the woods, it would be a longer one. Of course, he hadn't been in Seattle for a couple of years, but he imagined she was still around. There was a telephone in the restaurant; he used it to call a number etched in his memory; he never forgot anything.

A maid's voice answered, "Miz Houghton's residence."

Fargo said, "Let me speak to Mrs. Houghton."

"She still asleep."

"Wake her up. Tell her it's Neal Fargo."

"She be mad do I do that."

"She'll be a hell of a lot madder if you don't. Now, do what I say."

A moment's hesitation; then she yielded. There was silence; then a woman's voice, drowsy, silken with sleep, yet excited, too. "Neal! Is that really you?"

"Hello, Lynne. How you doing?"

"Ahhh — " He could imagine her stretching luxuriously beneath the satin sheets. "Much better, thank you, now that I hear your voice again. What a delightful surprise to wake up to. Will you join me for breakfast?"

Fargo's wolf's smile twisted his ugly features. "Why not? Three-quarters of an hour?"

"That'll be just about right."

"I'll see you, then."

"Be on time, darling." She chuckled softly. "And everything will be hot for you."

"I'll be there," Fargo said. "Goodbye," He hung up.

A trolley took him up hills to a fashionable section of town. The apartment house was large, expensive, and, on its top floor, Lynne Houghton's flat was a reflection of herself. The living room into which he was admitted was furnished in gilt and white, utterly luxurious, the carpet deep and soft under Fargo's boots, the crimson draperies shutting out the sunlight.

The maid ran approving eyes over Fargo's tall frame, his hard face.

"Miz Houghton in the bedroom," she murmured. "This way, if you please."

"I know where it is," Fargo said, grinning, and went to it. He knocked once, sharply. That silken voice said, "Come in."

The bed was enormous. The girl who lay in it was lovely. Her hair, let down, spilled over her shoulders in a golden stream, framing a face ivory white, its features cleanly chiseled and patrician, eyes huge and blue, lips full and red. She wore a nightgown and peignoir of nearly transparent apricot, frothy with lace. The room smelled excitingly of perfume. There was a table by the bed on which were covered dishes, a pot of coffee and a tea pot. At the sight of Fargo, Lynne Houghton's eyes flared smokily, the red lips curved. "Hello, Neal," she said huskily.

He went to her, bent, kissed her, and her mouth opened beneath his hungrily. Her hand came up to caress the back of his neck. The kiss lasted a long time. When it was over she sank back against heaped pillows the color of her nightdress and gave a shuddering sigh, large, rounded breasts rising and falling beneath the clinging silk, her nipples making little tents in the fabric. "Mmm," she murmured. "You've improved with age."

"So have you," Fargo sat down beside her on the bed. She took his hand, pressed it against the soft flesh of her bosom.

"It's been ages since I've heard from you," she said accusingly in that husky voice. "Why didn't you write?"

"I don't write many letters. Besides, where I've been, they're hard to mail."

Her brows went up. "Not in prison?"

He laughed. "Nope. That's the one place I've missed. But . . . Mexico, Panama, the Philippines, Alaska . . . "

"Umm? Business must have been good."

"Fine. How about you?"

She laughed. "You and I — we're like undertakers. What we sell never goes out of style."

He backed off a little, looked at her. She would be twenty-seven, maybe a little more, now. He had first known her in Rhyolite, a hell-roaring Nevada mining town, eight or nine years ago when she had lived in poverty, daughter of a broken-down prospector. Death Valley had got him; it had been a full year after he'd vanished before his skeleton was found, its leg bone broken, an empty canteen beside it. Meanwhile, she'd been left stranded. Fargo, dealing faro, had taken her in; she had, for a while, been his mistress. But the time had come when he had to move on — and he always traveled light, never liking to be hampered by a woman. As it turned out he had not needed to worry about her; she could take care of herself. Just before he pulled out, Cal Houghton hit town, a grizzled prospector who had just made a fantastic silver strike. He spotted the young girl, wanted her, got her — marriage license and all. He'd sold out his claim for a fortune;

they'd moved to Seattle, a good place to maintain contact with a venture or two in Alaska that he'd put money in. A year later he was dead, his old heart unable to take the strain of the high life of a rich man with a young and lusty wife — and Lynne Houghton was heiress to a fortune.

She had spent hardly any of it. There were plenty of men in Seattle with money — and she liked men and money. She could juggle two or three rich lovers at once, with each thinking he was paying the tab exclusively for the life of luxury she liked. But when Fargo hit town all bets were off for as long as he was around; there was something in her that still responded to the hard-bitten fighting man — a streak of wildness, of outlawry — that made it amusing to her to hoard her own money and take what she needed off of others.

Now her hand closed over his. She nodded toward the table, "Breakfast's ready. Coffee's hot — among other things." Smiling, she added, "If you want it."

"Maybe you're hungry," Fargo said.

"I am. But — " Her fingers stroked his hand. "Not for breakfast."

"Then let it wait," said Fargo. He arose, took off the coat, the shoulder holster, the shirt . . . She lay back in the bed, watching him with smoky eyes as he undressed, "How long will you be in town?"

"Just today," he said, and then he was in beside her.

"Ohh . . . " There was disappointment in her voice. "Well, then — we'll make today count for all we can."

"That was sort of what I figured. Come here," Fargo said. She did, sliding easily, quickly; she had shrugged out of the peignoir and the gown was open. Warm flesh molded itself against him, her mouth opened, seeking his . . .

★ ★ ★

Later, they drank coffee, and she ate a small breakfast of toast and bacon. Then they went back to bed. After that, they drank brandy. Then there was another interlude. Presently, as the afternoon wore on, Lynne arose, dressed in a gown of blue silk that hugged every line and curve of her figure. She was like a great cat that had eaten a big and satisfying canary as she leaned back against the curve of the sofa in the living room, while Fargo squirted water from a seltzer bottle into drinks of bonded bourbon. He handed her a glass, then from his pants, thumbed out a large gold watch. It was of the sort used by railroad men, durable and absolutely accurate. Sometimes even a second, much less a minute, could make a lot of difference in his business. "One hour," he said. "Then I'll have to be on my way."

"Where?"

"Up north." The rest of it was none of her business.

She smiled, inhaling smoke from her

cigarette. "The Wolf's Head Tract?"

Fargo turned, staring with narrowed eyes. "How'd you know?"

"A girl who lives like I do hears a lot." Then she was serious. "Fargo — "

"Yes." Something in her voice made him frown, watchful, alert.

"In a minute or two, we'll be having company."

He instinctively hooked a thumb in the shoulder harness of the Colt. "Who?"

Lynne sat up. "Saul Lasher."

For a moment Fargo was silent. Then he said, "Well, goddamn you."

"Don't be mad at me. It means no trouble for you. He called right after you did this morning. Said you were in town, he knew you'd be seeing me — "

"How did he know about us."

Lynne shrugged. "Pillow talk. He — comes here often."

"One of your strings, eh?" Fargo's voice rasped.

"If you want to put it that way, yes. Anyhow, he asked if I'd let him know when you were here. He wanted to talk to you."

"I've got nothing to talk to him about," Fargo tossed off half the drink. "He tried to have me killed last night."

"Not Saul!" She sounded shocked.

"Hell, yes, Saul."

"Well, he's not here for any fight or argument now. He said he had a business proposition — " She broke off as there was a loud, peremptory knock at the door. Then she jumped to her feet. "That'll be him now. Neal, please." She put a hand on his arm. "All he wants you to do is listen to him. Please don't — fight."

Fargo let out a long breath. Then he grinned coldly. "I won't if he don't. And I don't imagine he will; he'd rather hire his fighting done. All right, Lynne. Let the bastard in."

"Maybe it was wrong," she said, "but — I couldn't deny him the favor." She turned away, went to the door.

"Hello, honey," said a deep masculine voice.

65

"Saul." Then, almost warningly, "he's here."

"Fargo? Fine." Saul Lasher entered. Just inside the doorway he halted. "Neal," he said. "Good to see you again."

The logging game bred big men, hard men. Lasher was both, about Fargo's age, about his size. He wore tailor-made business clothes but the rippling muscles beneath them were almost too much for them to contain. He was strikingly handsome, eyes as gray as Fargo's own and quite as steady, his black hair frosted slightly at the temples, his smile, so unlike Fargo's wolf snarl, charming, friendly. What marred the image was a scar down one side of Lasher's face, left there by the blade of a double-bit ax in a wild lumber camp fight. Rumor had it that Lasher's own stroke in return had beheaded his opponent like a guillotine.

But that had been in a different era, when Lasher'd been a woods boss.

Now he was a business man, wealthy, with connections in the Governor's office and in Washington. He was smooth but wary as he came forward, hand out.

"Hello, Saul." Fargo took the hand, shook it briefly. It was not hard any longer; good living had softened a palm once calloused and tough as horn.

The room was silent for a moment. Then Lasher took the drink Lynne handed him. "How long's it been? Four years? Not since the Salmon Rapids."

"That's right," Fargo said.

"You beat me out that time," Lasher said without a trace of rancor. "We were both driving the same river, a race to hit the mills first, skim the cream off a rising market."

"Uh huh. And you used every trick in the book to try to balk us."

"Oh, come now, Neal. All's fair in love, war, and the timber business." he sat down, crossed his legs. "I understand you're going back into it."

"News travels fast."

67

"A fight like that one with Hotchkiss last night becomes a sort of landmark. It'll be remembered for years — another part of the legend of Neal Fargo." His eyes changed, losing their good humor, opaque now. "Lynne — honey, would you excuse us?"

She hesitated, looked at Fargo. He nodded. "Yes, I've got to do something with my hair, anyhow." She touched it lightly with one hand though it was perfectly arranged, and went into the bedroom.

When she had shut the door, Lasher took out two cigars, handed Fargo one, clamped the other between his teeth. When they were lit, he blew smoke. "You'll notice I'm not making any issue of your being — here."

"Issue?" Fargo grinned. "You couldn't stop me from seeing Lynne. Or her from seeing me."

"Exactly. That's why I'm not making any issue of it, though she's my girl — usually. I accept realities, Fargo. Actually, I'm glad of this chance to

68

meet you in private, have a little talk. You're signed on with Great Northwestern."

"That's right. Duke hired me as a faller."

Lasher's mouth twisted. He said a terse obscenity. "Faller. You mean that's your cover."

"I'm working in the woods for pay," answered Fargo smoothly. "Same as any other timber beast."

Lasher snorted. "All right. If that's the case, you must need money. Maybe you'd be receptive to an offer."

"What kind of offer?" Fargo rolled the cigar across his mouth.

Lasher hesitated. "Twenty-five thousand dollars. To work for me instead of MacKenzie."

"Where?"

"On the Wolf's Head."

Fargo smiled. "You don't operate on the Wolf's Head."

"Ah. But come next spring, I will." Lasher's face was intent. "Damn it, Fargo, I know you. With you, money talks. And you know me. When I name a sum, that's as good as cash in the bank."

"And what I'd have to do for it — ?"

"Is nothing. Long as you're on Wolf's Head, absolutely nothing except earn lumberjack's wages as a faller. Stay out of everything else. I don't care what you're drawing from MacKenzie. You do nothing while you're out there but cut down trees and you'll get twenty-five thousand from me — half now, half when I take over the Wolf's Head Tract."

Fargo took the cigar from his mouth, stood up. "You sure are scared of me, Saul"

"I've seen you operate before. It's worth the money to have you on my side. Well, Neal?"

Fargo picked up his coat, fished in the pocket. he brought out the snub-nosed gun, jacked the loads from it. "This is something that belongs to you, Saul. Catch."

Instinctively, Lasher caught the little

gun. "What the hell — ?"

"Last night you tried the cheap way. It didn't work. Today you try the expensive one." Fargo's voice roughened. "It still won't work, Saul. It might have if you had got me soon enough, but you're a day late and a dollar short. Besides, when you try to murder me, you git my hackles up. I don't know how much you paid the gunman, but that little Colt's all you git back for your investment."

Shortly, coldly, then, he laughed. "I'm loggin' for MacKenzie. Cuttin' wood's like punchin' cows; you hire on to a brand, you fight for it long as it pays your wages. Against anybody, Saul, and everybody. Remember that."

Lasher arose, hand caressing the Banker's Special, big thumb turning the empty cylinder around and around. His eyes met Fargo's, and they were hard and dangerous. "All right, Neal. But don't forget. I came up in a hard school. I know how to play rough, too. Go ahead and back MacKenzie. And sign your death warrant at the same time." He thrust the gun into his pocket, wheeled. "Don't say I didn't warn you, Fargo."

Fargo said, "Lasher, I'll keep everything you've said in mind. Believe me, I'll keep it in mind."

Lasher didn't answer. He only strode out, slamming the door behind him.

Fargo stood there, staring at it for a moment. Then, from the bedroom, Lynne emerged. "Neal, what was that — ?"

"End of a business discussion," said Fargo.

Lynne Houghton blinked. Then she took his arm. "I don't know what's between Saul and you, but right now it doesn't matter. Not to me. Neal, the day's not over — "

Fargo sighed. "No. It's just beginning. Before long, the crew'll pull out for Wolf's Head. Sorry, honey."

She looked at him. After a moment, she said: "No, you're not. You've got what you came for. Now you want something else. Damn you, Neal."

"That's the way I'm built," he grinned. Then he kissed her long and hard. "Goodbye. See you after the fall drive." He turned toward the door.

Her voice stopped him short. "Neal."

"Yeah?" Hand on the knob, he looked at her.

Lynne's eyes were huge and serious. "Neal — come back."

He nodded. "I aim to," he said. "So long." Then he went out and closed the door behind him.

4

THEY left Seattle at six o'clock that afternoon, riding north in darkness on the daycoaches of a little train — forty lumberjacks, their quarterly blast in town over now, most of them with freshly-emptied pockets and surly with hangovers. At midnight they disembarked at a hamlet high in the hills where wagons drawn by mule teams waited. The hangovers were not helped by the jolting over rough roads which had been corduroyed in spots. As always in such circumstances, Fargo slept while he could, like a huge cat, gathering rest.

Higher into the mountains they climbed, the mules straining in their harness. Daybreak found them in big timber but it had been cut over. In the gray light Fargo judged that this was the beginning of the Wolf's Head;

74

the cutting had been selective and good stands of smaller trees were left to reseed and preserve the wilderness.

Then they descended into a valley swirling with mist. As it cleared briefly, Fargo saw the logging camp below them: five long log bunkhouses in a semi-circle, a cookshack, mess-hall, office and tool sheds. Beyond the Wolf's Head River had been dammed and a chute ran down its steep flank into the big pond thus formed. There, cut logs floated in rafts, waiting until there was enough accumulated timber to warrant blowing the dam and starting the drive.

Men came awake as the wagons rattled down the hill, stopped in the middle of the camp. From the lead wagon Duke Hotchkiss leaped down, clad in mackinaw, stagged pants, caulked boots. "Awright, you farmers!" he bellowed at the dozing men. "Daybreak in the swamps. Roust out! You got two hours to git settled and eat; then we start highballin'."

Beside Fargo, a young, blocky redhead with wide shoulders beneath his mackinaw grinned sourly. "Good ole Duke, he's all heart." He picked up a bedroll, slung it over his shoulder. "You need help with that trunk, feller?"

"I can manage." Fargo jumped from the wagon, hooked one strap of the trunk with a hand and carried it easily on his shoulder, his other hand occupied with rolled blankets. The redhead leaped down beside him. "That's a might big turkey."

A turkey was what loggers called a man's bag of possessions. The man went on, full of curiosity. "What you got in there — crown jools?"

"Somethin' like that."

"My name's Milligan, Jerry Milligan. I'm a faller on Side Number Three."

"Fargo. I'm hired on as faller, too."

"Good. Likely you and me'll work together." Milligan's grin vanished. "There's a vacancy. I lost my partner jest before we got paid off and went outside."

76

"Lost him?" Fargo looked sharply at Milligan as they entered a bunkhouse. He set the trunk down, stowed it under a bunk next to the one on which Milligan tossed his bedroll.

"That's right." Milligan nodded. "But nothin' I could help. In fact, we ain't figgered out yet how it happened. We found him floatin' out there in the pond one mornin'. All we can make out is that he musta tried to cross on the logs in the dark and fell in and a log bounced up against him and crushed his skull."

"What was he doin' crossin' the river in the dark?" Fargo untied his bedroll, spread his blankets on the cheap straw mattress.

"That's what we don't know. Maybe goin' for a walk, maybe — " Milligan smirked " — he figgered on tryin' his luck with Barbara."

"Barbara? Oh, you mean the Government Inspector's daughter."

"You've heard about her, huh?" Milligan whistled, made an expressive curving gesture with his hands. "Yeah, Charlie Ross always did figger himself as God's gift to women. She and her daddy live over across the river in the clearin', out of camp where she won't be exposed to us roughnecks. That's supposed to be off-limits to us, but Charlie, he'd git a sniff of perfume and away he'd go and to hell with everything." Then he sobered. "Expensive sniff."

Other men were spreading out their beds. Milligan dropped his voice. "That ain't been the only accident, either. I tell you, Fargo, Duke's a good boss, but this seems to be a jinxed job. You got to watch your step around here. I never seen so many men killed or crippled on one operation in all my life. And no accountin' for it. Duke takes every safety precaution, right by the book, and these are all experienced men, no greenhorns. And still, there's always somethin' happenin'."

He straightened up, moved closer to Fargo, his pale blue eyes serious.

"There's somethin' in the air. You know how it is when there's a forest fire a long ways off, a big one, a crown fire roarin' through the tree tops? Even miles away, when you can't really see it or smell the smoke, you know it's there, a kind of stingin' in your nose, a taste on your tongue. Whatever is goin' on here is like that — like a crown fire." He spat into the sandbox under the cold stove in the center of the room. "I reckon I'm spooky. I swore when we went out to Seattle that I wasn't coming back in to the Wolf's Head. I changed my mind but now I wish I hadn't. Seems like to me I can feel and taste whatever it is all over again, and it scares me."

"Loggin's always dangerous," Fargo said.

"Sure. Maybe that's it. Maybe I'm just losin' my nerve. All I know is I've worked from New Brunswick to Maine to North Michigan and all through Oregon and Washin'ton, and I ain't felt like this since the Tillamook Burn started and looked like it was gonna burn up the whole Northwest. Well, hell, let's go eat."

★ ★ ★

The mess-hall was big, with trestle tables. The bullcook — cook's helper, swamper, and general man of all work — was kept busy hauling platters laden with food. Meals in a lumber camp were always enormous, and with good reason. Fargo stuffed himself, well knowing how much fuel a man could burn in a hard day's work in the Douglas fir.

Then the meal was over; Hotchkiss slammed on the end table and jumped to his feet. "All right, you hay-shakers! Playtime's over, it's back to work. We got to git out a pile of timber between now and the drive and anybody I see doggin' it, I'll take apart in little bitty pieces and forgit to put him back together again! Side One and Two, move out! Side Three, we're gonna re-rig and start a new cut. Fargo, you're on Side Three, workin' with Milligan. Stick with him and he'll show you around!"

The men filed out of the mess-hall, went to the tool houses, were issued tools by the clerk. Between them, Fargo and Milligan drew two double-bit axes, a file, wedges, a crosscut saw, and a small can of kerosene. The mist had lifted and Fargo got a better view of the surroundings. Mountains towered all around them clad in a thick shag of fir. Roads spiked out in all directions from the camp, penetrating the cut-over woods. The men of the first two sides piled into wagons, were hauled into the forest. In the distance Fargo heard the sputtering snort and then slow, steady thunder of donkey engines.

Other wagons were brought up. With Hotchkiss and ten other men, Fargo and Milligan loaded up. The last one to climb aboard was a lean, wiry man of about thirty, who, despite the fact that he stood nearly six-feet six, moved as smoothly and fluidly as a cat. He carried a belt and a coiled rope over one arm, stowed ax and saw, and put on top of them a pair of climbing irons, brace-like frames to fit over his boots, long spikes, razor-sharp to bite into the wood of a tree trunk. Fargo recognized immediately the gear of the high-climber.

Milligan introduced them. "Chuck Hoskins, Neal Fargo."

Hoskins' hand was hard and strong; the tremendous muscles required for his job — the hardest, most dangerous in logging — rippled under his shirt. But his smile was warm, friendly, and unassuming. "Glad to know you, Fargo." Then his eyes widened, "Ah hah, looks like we got company."

Fargo followed the direction of his gaze. Two riders had splashed across the shallows below the dam; now their horses crested the edge of the bank and loped toward the wagons. One was a burly man in his mid-forties, in a battered Forest Service hat, not unlike Fargo's cavalry hat, mackinaw, and jodhpurs. The girl beside him wore a jacket, tight blue jeans, and her coppery hair glinted in the sun. When they pulled up alongside the wagon Fargo got a better look at her and whistled soundlessly.

Jonah, Hotchkiss had said. *Right*, Fargo thought. *Any girl that looks like that in a camp full of horny men is about the worst bad medicine there is.*

As if to underscore the thought, she took off her jacket and stuffed it between her thighs and the saddle horn, as Fargo's eyes raked over big round breasts bulging against a shirt just a shade too tight — and deliberately so. He heard Milligan make a sound in his throat, and Hoskins was beginning to wear a silly smile. "Hello, Miss Mannix," he said.

She looked at the men in the wagon and smiled back. Her hair was indeed the color of copper, with maybe a tinge of gold. Her forehead was high, eyes huge and sea-green, with long lashes; her skin ivory, her nose short and straight, her mouth lush and red. She drew in a breath that made the breasts move under the straining fabric, shifted one superb leg, not an inch of its outline blurred by denim that might have been painted on. "Hello, boys," She sat like that, almost posing, for a second more — giving us all a thrill, Fargo thought wryly — and then she spurred up to rein in beside her father.

"Thought I'd be on hand when you start the new side, Duke." Mannix's voice was deep. "Barbara always likes to watch the high-climber work, anyhow."

"That's the Government Inspector," Milligan whispered to Fargo. "Forest Service."

"Glad to have yuh, Mannix," Hotchkiss rumbled. "Okay, let's move out!"

The wagons lumbered ahead. They entered a road that led through forest where raw stumps gleamed — the butts of giant firs that had taken hundreds of years to attain their soaring heights of up to two hundred feet. Now they were gone, to be turned into houses for an exploding population that, Fargo thought bitterly, was eating up the wilderness like a bunch of termites. Or like sheep, he thought with the wolf's contempt for animals that could be herded. Again Fargo felt sympathy with The Colonel's concern for the cutting of this tract. When he'd been President, The Colonel had, in 1907, established the first system of National Forests, setting aside sixteen million acres in six far Western states. This was part of it; The Colonel hated to see it logged at all, but if it had to be logged, better that it be done right.

Hotchkiss and MacKenzie had been doing it right so far. They'd got the timber out, Fargo noted, with the minimum amount of destruction of the remaining woods. Again his mouth twisted, thinking of what he knew of

Saul Lasher's method of operation. This vast tract of fir was worth a fortune but it would be worth double to Lasher what MacKenzie would get from it. Lasher would cut everything that could possibly be worth a nickle and rip up the rest getting out his cut. That way he'd double MacKenzies quarter of a million, maybe triple it — and a man like Saul Lasher would stop at nothing for money like that. Fargo knew what Milligan had meant. Along with the sharp, clean tang of fir, it seemed to him he could smell trouble, bitter and acrid, like the taint of a distant, invisible fire . . .

As the wagon lurched over the rough road, straining uphill, then banging down steep slopes, the girl let her mount drop back slightly. She wanted to give the men another good look at her, Fargo guessed. He took one, raking his eyes insolently over her from head to toe, letting them pause at the bouncing breasts joggling to the gait of her horse, the rounded rump planted in the saddle. She felt the pressure of his eyes, and when he looked up again her own were fastened on his scarred and ugly face. Something seemed to swirl in them as he met them directly, and he thought she smiled faintly, and not without invitation.

Presently they entered a level, cut-over clearing of considerable size within a great, forested bowl. Here sat the yarder, a big donkey engine on skids, its several drums wound with heavy cables. Its operator and fireman had already gotten up steam and it was chugging rhythmically.

"We'll skid the yarder into place first!" Duke called out as the teams stopped. After that, for a long time, the morning was a nightmare.

The loggers had eaten out all the timber around the clearing. The spar tree, naked now of the blocks and cables that had formerly been rigged on it, towered nearly two hundred feet into the air. Presently it would be taken down, converted into lumber, but for the moment it would still be needed, later. Meanwhile, the donkey engine had to be gotten to the new location where the cutting was to take place.

That was accomplished by letting it winch itself along with its own cables, fastened to trees ahead of it. But a path had to be cleared for it, and, as Hotchkiss had warned, this country was all straight up and down. They spent four hours moving the donkey, downhill and up, with Duke yelling and driving like a madman and Fargo re-establishing his acquaintance with an ax and cross cut.

He was thoroughly expert with both, but they used special muscles, certain ones he had not called into play in years. He knew he had put in a morning's work by the time Hotchkiss was satisfied. When the wagon from the cookshack came with hot tea and coffee and huge meat sandwiches, he was ready for the chow. Soaked in sweat, he sat cross-legged with Milligan and Hoskins under a huge fir and wolfed the food ravenously.

Then a shadow fell across him, and, surprisingly, he thought he caught a tinge of perfume. He looked up to see Barbara Mannix standing over them, cup in one hand, sandwich in the other. "Hello, boys," she said in a deep and husky voice. "Would it jinx you if I ate here?"

Milligan blinked his eyes. "Duke might not like it much . . . "

She laughed and sat down cross-legged, soft flesh of thighs straining at the tight denim. "I can handle Duke." Her green eyes went to Fargo. "You're new."

"That's right." He met her gaze levelly.

"White haired. You're not that old."

"I've led a hard life." he said.

She nodded, almost seriously. "I'll bet you have. You look it. You look tough as nails. Funny, though. Those legs of yours. You look more like a rider than a lumberjack."

"I've done a lot of things in my

time," said Fargo.

"And will probably do more," She smiled, showing small white teeth. Then she turned to Hoskins, who immediately smiled that silly grin again.

"Chuck, you're going to put on a show?"

"Well, ma'am, I'm gonna top a spar tree if that's a show."

"It's the best show I know of." She put out a hand, touched his belt and coiled rope and spikes. "To go two hundred feet up, work there with nothing to hold you but these. I'd love to try it sometime. I don't know how you can possibly do it." She finished her sandwich, washed it down with a swallow of coffee and set down her cup. She picked up one of the heavy climbing irons. "How does it go on?" she asked, trying to fit her own booted foot into it. "Like this?"

"You've got it wrong side to," said Hoskins, his lean face brick red.

"Then show me the right way. Maybe

someday I'll be the world's only female high-climber." She smiled at Fargo. "You see, I'm sort of the mascot of this outfit."

"I can imagine," said Fargo thinly.

But Hoskins had laid his food aside. When Barbara Mannix held out one small foot, he almost leaped at the opportunity to show her how the climbing iron should fit. He lashed it into place.

She held up the other foot. "Now, the left one."

He put that one on, too. She got to her feet awkwardly, holding her legs apart to clear the in-pointed spikes. The way she stood emphasized the swell of buttocks beneath the denim, and Fargo heard Hoskins draw in a quick breath. Barbara bent, picked up the leather tool belt and the rope. "Show me how this works."

"Chuck," said Jerry Milligan warningly, with a glance toward Duke Hotchkiss. But the Duke was hunkered down with the girl's father, deep in conversation. Hoskins disregarded Milligan; his huge hands shook as he buckled the heavy belt around the girl's slender waist, showed her how to snap on one end of the climbing rope.

She ran her hands along it, then went to a small spruce nearby. "Like this?" She looped the rope around the trunk, latched the other end. Then, wrapping her arms around the tree, she tried to sink in the spike, failed, fell back, laughing, into Hoskins' waiting arms. Fargo did not miss how she leaned into his embrace for a split second longer than necessary to gain her balance. Then she straightened up, pulled free. "Unharness me, Chuck. I'll never make a high-climber."

No, thought Fargo, but you tried hard enough.

When she had the gear off she sat down again and drained the coffee cup. "Don't you get afraid so high in the air?" she asked Hoskins. "What would happen if the rope broke?"

He grinned, "I might come down

awful quick. But that rope ain't gonna break. I checked it this mornin' myself; I always check it every mornin', even if I did the night before. It'll hold an elephant. The only thing I got to worry about is accidentally cuttin' it when I'm trimmin' limbs."

"Aren't you afraid of that?"

Hoskins laughed. "Not hardly. I been toppin' timber fer nearly fifteen years. I ain't come close yet."

The girl's face turned serious. "All the same, Chuck," and she put a hand on his, "be careful when you're up there. Sometimes my heart just stops when I see you up there; it stops and doesn't start again until you're down safely."

Hoskins' face reddened deeper. "Golly, Miss Barbara — "

"Barbara!" The summons rang out clearly in the noon silence. Mannix had gotten to his feet. He strode over to her, and Fargo saw him close up for the first time. He saw angry black eyes beneath heavy brows, a nose like a blade, the thin blue veins of the drinking man webbed through the cheeks, the mouth like a slash. Mannix seized his daughter's wrist, jerked her roughly to her feet. "Listen — " His fierce eyes swept over the trio, Fargo, Milligan, and Hoskins without apology for the interruption. "You know what I told you!"

"Dad!" She twisted in his grasp. "You're hurting me."

"I'll hurt you worse if you don't start listening to what I tell you." He shoved her roughly across the clearing in which they had halted, sat her down hard beside the tethered horses. "You stay there." She looked after him with swirling eyes as he went back to Hotchkiss, squatted, and they conferred for a moment more.

Then the Duke jumped to his feet. "All right, you plow-jockys! You've had your break! Time to hit the woods!"

5

AN hour later they were in virgin timber. The huge firs soared up on every side. One among them was a giant, towering fifty feet above its fellows.

Duke pointed toward its top. "There," he said. "That's our spar."

Hoskins looped upward, nodded, cooly spat tobacco juice. "Right enough. She's a beauty."

She was indeed, Fargo thought. Rig an enormous bull-block up there at its top, run heavy cables through it and the other rigging, cinch the chokers feeding off of them around the timber the fallers would cut down and the buckers cut up into thirty or forty-foot lengths, let the yarder man reel in his cables, and you could walk a long stick of timber through thc trees at the end of a cable like a big fish being hauled in on a line. Re-rig to another cable, another spar and keep it walking until it reached the bank of the Wolf's Head where it would slide down the chute and join its fellows for the drive. Mechanized logging, high-lead logging. About the only way to get the timber out of such mountains, and a far cry from the old days of skidding each stick out behind straining mules or oxen.

But even more dangerous than the old method. In the old days, there were no steel cables under high tension that might snap, chopping down any thing of flesh in their paths. No boilers to blow, no high-climbing . . . Add those to the dangers of falling trees and glancing axes, combine the hell-for-leather business of balancing on a log while it swirled down a roaring stream at flood time, and you had the most dangerous industry in the world. Even under the best of circumstances logging killed men or crippled them; and this, everyone had said, was a jinxed job.

But if Hoskins had any reservations

he didn't show them. Until he topped the spar tree there was nothing for the rest of the crew to do; besides, this was a show that all were entitled to watch. Fargo admired the coolness with which the tall man strapped on his climbing irons, cinched on his belt, fastening ax and saw, and locked the end of the safety rope before he threw it around the gigantic trunk. Fargo had faced nearly every imaginable danger in all parts of the world but the only thing that truly frightened him was height. He had an inborn fear of high places. It was something instinctive that he had trained himself to overcome but, even mastering it, he never felt at home high up. He had done high-climbing himself and for all he knew, he might be as expert at it as Hoskins. But for him it was a serious matter requiring a supreme act of will, while Hoskins, obviously indifferent to height, might have been getting duded up for a Sunday afternoon drive with his girl.

Now Chuck accepted the other end

of the safety rope, which was also an aid in climbing such an enormous trunk. Hotchkiss handed it to him and Chuck fastened it tightly, and then all conversation died as he raised a leg, took a strain, and sank the climbing iron on his right leg into the soft fir. Then, like a monkey or a telephone lineman going up a pole, he climbed.

His speed was fantastic, and the hush over the clearing persisted as he scaled seventy feet up to the lower branches. Fargo's eyes flickered to Barbara Mannix across the clearing beside her father. Her face was turned up, her breasts rose and fell magnificently under her shirt. Danger, Fargo thought. Danger stoked her furnace. He grinned wryly, then watched Hoskins again.

Now the high-climber had reached the first branches. He leaned back against the rope, balanced on his spikes; the ax-blade gleaming as he began to chip. The first small limbs drifted to earth.

Chuck went higher. Now the branches

were bigger. But he was expert with his tools and unconcerned about working almost a hundred feet above the ground. He was, thought Fargo, who knew the demands this work made, a genius at his trade. Huge limbs were crashing down now, their butts as thick as the very trunks of shade trees on the lawns of people who lived in town. Ax and saw, ax and saw . . . Slowly Hoskins cleared the trunk. Now he was hardly more than forty feet from the top. Another twenty and he'd halt, cut off the limber end of the trunk — and then would come the time of maximum danger. Nearly two hundred feet up, if he misjudged his cut, the tree top pitched the wrong way, crashed down upon him — well, then, Fargo thought, he was finished.

He was glad that tiny figure up there moving monkey-like was Hoskins and not himself.

Chuck moved up another three feet. Now a huge limb blocked his way. He unslung his ax, got ready for a beginning cut. Fargo saw the double-bitted blade gleam as it swung out, chopping in. The blade moved rhythmically, a shining arc, too fast for the eye to follow . . .

Then something happened, Fargo had no idea what, Chuck was cutting too fast to tell. But something. He saw the long, lean body give a strange lurch. Then Hoskins reached out with one hand, desperately trying to embrace the trunk. He missed his grip; the ax dropped, came hurtling down. Then Fargo saw the loose end of the severed rope flashing.

"Jesus Christ," breathed Milligan. "He cut his climbin' rope!"

The chopped rope fell free. Now Hoskins hugged with both arms, but he was off balance, had been, in mid-stroke. Inexorably, his own weight threw him outward. He turned on the climbing spikes as if they were an axle. He hung head downward. They heard him scream.

Then he fell.

He screamed all the way down.

More than one hundred and fifty feet.

His body made a sickening sound when it landed in the forest duff.

Barbara Mannix screamed, too. She had, Fargo realized, been screaming as Hoskins fell, and she went on screaming when he hit.

All the men rushed forward. Fargo shoved past the others, reached the inner circle around what had been Chuck Hoskins as Duke Hotchkiss bent over the mangled body. Fargo saw the one leg had been totally twisted and fractured; the razor-sharp climbing spike had come up on its weirdly cramped length and was rammed through Hoskins' belly. But that had not been what killed him. The fall had done that.

Duke looked down at his man with a strangely impassive face. Then a touch of sadness registered as he stood up. "Good God," he husked. "An old hand like him cutting his own climbing rope.

Good God . . . " He shook his head, turned away, back to Fargo. Fargo saw the broad, enormous shoulders tremble. But when the Duke turned, his face was hard, composed.

"That tears it," he said. "We can't open up this Side until I can get back to Seattle and hire another high-climber." He struck his iron-hard thigh. "Goddammit! Another four, five days delay, anyhow, for a third of our operation. And as bad as we need to pile up the timber — " His eyes swept over the crew. "But there ain't another high-climber in the whole damned camp!"

For Fargo, it was almost as if a great hand propelled him forward. "Yes," he heard himself say. "There is."

Duke started at him. "You? You can top a spar tree?"

"I've done it before."

"It's no job for an amateur," Duke rapped.

"I ain't," said Fargo, "an amateur."

Hotchkiss kept on staring. "You

mean you want to go up there?" He
gestured.

"When we get another climbing
rope," said Fargo.

"There are climbing ropes back at
camp."

"I know," said Fargo. He told
himself that he was a fool. But the
thing about it was he'd hired out
to make MacKenzie's cutting of the
Wolf's Head a success. Whatever that
required. He'd given his word to The
Colonel."

Then he gestured to the limp body.
"Take his irons and safety belt off him.
I'll be back directly." He strode toward
Barbara Mannix. "Miss Mannix, can I
borrow your horse?"

She stared at him with unreadable
eyes. Then, mutely, she nodded.

"Thanks," said Fargo, and he swung
into the saddle without touching stirrup.

He rode the animal hard. It was
lathered when he reached the logging
camp. He drew another climbing rope
from the clerk, inspected it minutely,

103

satisfied himself that it was sound, looped it around the saddle horn, and put the tired animal back into the woods. When he reached the clearing and swung down, the horse was dead beat, standing with head dropping between its legs, sides heaving like bellows.

Duke's eyes were incredulous. "You made good time."

"I know how to ride," Fargo said. He turned to Barbara. "Walk him for a while. He'll be all right if you walk him for half an hour." Then he looked back at Duke. "The irons," he said. "The safety belt."

They had been taken off of Hoskins' corpse which had been laid out under the branches of a grove. Fargo examined them as carefully as he had scrutinized the climbing rope. Milligan came up to him. "You want some help?"

"Nobody," Fargo snapped, "touches this gear but me! Nobody!"

Then he was satisfied. He hooked the wire-bound loop of one end of the safety rope into the toggle on the belt, made sure it was locked. He confronted the enormous fir trunk. Duke made a motion. "I'll pass the rope around to you."

"Keep your goddamn hands off that rope!" Fargo snarled. He was an expert with a lariat; he gave the rope a twist and its end hurtled around the trunk. He caught it, snapped it into the belt. With ax and saw dangling, heavy weights, he sucked in a long breath and began to climb.

He socked the tree hard with his strong legs. The spurs bit in. He tucked his body toward the trunk. Two steps at a time, he thought, then move the rope.

He did it that way. Two steps, move the rope, two more, go on up. Incredibly, he was forty, fifty feet off the ground before he knew it. The faces below were tiny blurs . . .

But now it was all coming back to him. He gained confidence. Don't look down, he thought; look up.

Above, the untopped spar towered, its shaggy head a challenge. Fargo's feet, finding rhythm and instinctive knowledge, socked in the climbing irons, deep and solid. He kept the rope moving.

Up, on up, past the fresh-cut knots that Chuck Hoskins, now crumpled fresh below, had chopped or sawed. On up, ten feet, twenty more. Don't look down . . . He was a hundred feet in the air, then. That instinctive fear, even though he saw nothing but the huge trunk before him, had clenched his gut. When you had watched a man you'd known come screaming down from a hundred and fifty feet up —

He went on relentlessly. What kept him going was the fact that he was doing a job. He had never hired out to do a job in his life that he had skimped or dogged. You didn't work for twenty thousand a throw if you operated that way. And death was death, whether it came from a rebel Mexican's bullet or when you hit the ground from this high up. It was all part of the game.

Then there were the branches, the ones Chuck had not had a chance to cut. They feathered over him, and his nostrils were full of the pungency of their needles and the bleeding pitch from those already severed. Fir pitch, a woods smell, a strong smell, the smell of work and danger. He was all right now. The rope would hold. He would have to be careful not to chop it. Maybe someday they'd wise up and put a metal core in a climbing rope, so such an accident could not happen, he thought.

He braced himself among the needled foliage, balanced on his spurs. He unhooked his ax, went to work. His muscles were loosened now by the morning's work. Occasionally, he glanced down. They were like ants below, white faces upward. Like little, tiny ants. He was up above them all. But he was still scared. He would bc, until solid ground was beneath his feet.

But the fact that he was scared, that he was forcing himself to do something almost beyond his powers felt good. This was how a man stayed a man, to keep moving out, doing things that scared him. This was how you knew you still had your balls. The ax rose and fell, accurately, with rhythm. Limbs crashed down. Fargo clutched the rope, lifted one spur, balancing on the other. Nearly two hundred feet high now, he climbed.

Then he had reached the spot.

Here was the pay-off; this was where the high-climber earned his money. From here on up the tree was too limber; it had to be topped. Here. One hundred and eighty, maybe two hundred, feet above the ground.

He leaned back out on the rope, pivoting on the irons. His eyes shot up the trunk which was arrow straight. He searched it for any deviation, for weight of foliage on any side. Because now, when he chopped and sawed off the top, his life depended on knowing which way it would fall. It had to fall away from him. If he misjudged, made the slightest mistake, if the butt kicked out and came down upon him, if it went to the side and the falling branches lashed him loose . . . No. No, this had to be perfect. Absolutely perfect. It was the only way he could keep alive.

His experienced gaze roved, judged. The limbs were heavier on yon side. The trunk had whip to it; when the top fell it would lash. He would have to know which way, be prepared for that. It was a hell of a job when you had been out of the woods as long as he had.

But there was no way out. He made his decision. Then he unslung his ax, began to chop his undercut on the side where he wanted the tree top to fall. He had to ease around to do that, manipulating rope and spurs with utmost cleverness and still trying not to look down, not to think about how long it would take a man to drop so far and what would go through his head while he did. The ax bit deeply, throwing large, pungent chips as Fargo chopped a clean cut.

Then it was right. Absolutely right, had to be. Another inch's cut might foul up everything. He worked the equation in his head, hooked the ax on the belt, unlimbered the saw, but only after he had worked back around the trunk to the far side from his ax cut.

Above him, twenty feet of treetop towered, and below him the onlookers — he cast his eyes down briefly, then was dizzy — were reduced to tiny grains. He started his cut, began to work the saw.

It bit deeply, pouring sweet-smelling grains of living tree across his poised, locked legs. He sawed, and sawed, body moving rhythmically, using all its strength. It seemed to him that he sawed forever.

Then he felt the motion in the tree. The trunk vibrated, began to whip and, instinctively, he dug in deeper with his spikes. The huge fir that had sprouted centuries before his birth let out a kind of gasping moan. Fibres ripped. The tree top wavered. Fargo stared up, fascinated, wondering which way it would go.

Then the butt kicked. The severed portion of the top lashed out just above his head. Overbalanced, it began to fall, ripping wood with it, making his rope jump. Then it was free, falling loosely.

Reaction. The whole tall stump of the Douglas fir began to whip. It lashed back and forth viciously, but Fargo had judged the probable direction and braced himself. As the cry rang out of his throat, "Timberrrrrrrr — " the great length of treetop hurtled down. He jerked the climbing rope up tight, gathering in slack, and hung on for dear life. It was like the mast of a ship in a heavy gale. Below, he heard a thunderous crash. Slowly, the trunk eased its motion. Fargo, hands sweating, held the rope tightly, kept tension on his ankles to drive the irons home.

Then the huge, raped tree had shuddered to a halt; it was still. Fargo let out a long breath. Almost timidly, he disengaged one iron and started the long climb downward.

★ ★ ★

Earth felt good beneath his feet. He savored its solidity, as Duke Hotchkiss pounded him on the back, "Fargo! Goddamn, Fargo, you did it!"

"Yeah," Fargo said thinly. Then he smelled again that waft of perfume. Barbara Mannix's hands clamped around his wrists, "Oh, Fargo, that was magnificent." He looked into those swirling green eyes, read what was written in them. The excitement, the invitation . . . He pulled his hands away, remembering how she'd handled Chuck Hoskin's climbing rope.

Duke moved between them. "When you're rested, you got to go back up, you know. We got to rig the guinea line, the bull-block, the haul back . . . "

"I know," said Fargo. "Gimme a minute."

He went off into the spruce, taking his gear with him so no one could tamper with it. He sat down there, smoked a cigarette. Then another. They calmed him. He came back to the base of the topped stub. The worst of it was over. "All right, Duke," he said. "I'm ready to go back up. Bring the gear."

It took him the rest of the afternoon to complete the rigging. When he was through, the forest was festooned with cables. Tomorrow they could start getting out the timber. No time was lost.

They buried Chuck Hoskins at sunset. If he had any relatives nothing in his turkey gave their name. His body was committed, without prayer or ceremony, to the rich earth of the Wolf's Head Tract. They put a wooden cross over his grave but the wet air of the coastal mountains would soon rot it down, obscure it with moss and fern. Fargo thought that maybe it was just as well. He had lived in the woods, let him die in them, become part of them.

He ate as hearty a supper as any of the rest. After chow they went into the bunkhouse, dried their socks and clothes and rehashed the long day, told tall tales of other jobs and of high-binding blasts in the timber towns. Fargo sat apart from them. He was in no mood for their loose talk. Some reaction had fastened a mood upon him. At half past eight, the last lamp was quenched. Before long the bunkhouse was full of variegated snores.

Fargo lay awake. When everyone else slept he arose, soundlessly as a cat. Dressed, pulled on boots. The air of the bunkhouse was steamy with the smells of masculinity; he wanted the clean scent of cut spruce. Clothed, he went out into the wet, chill darkness of the Washington highlands at the approach of fall.

He walked through the sleeping camp toward the river. He halted at the dam, stared down into the pond where a fortune in cut fir floated in the water. His eyes surveyed the dam, it was made of logs and stone, high and wide, with a relief spillway at the far side, cut too small to let through a saleable spruce log. The water pounded, thundered, over the spillway. Something about the dam bothered Fargo. After a while, he knew what it was.

Charlie Ross.

God's gift to women, Milligan had said; and Ross had died trying to cross that swirling, brawling river on the logs. But that was foolish, that was absurd. The dam itself made a fine bridge across the river. No lumberjack worth his salt would balk at jumping the sixfoot spillway. Why hadn't Ross crossed on the dam instead of on the log boom?

Maybe he had, Fargo thought, and

he eased down the bank, onto the dam's solid top.

He felt the vibration of angry, penned water behind the structure. Come time to drive, blow this dam, those logs would go swirling downstream like race horses on a track, especially in fall flood. He came to the spillway, it's gap did not seem challenging. He leaped it. Landed, cat-like, on the other side.

He climbed the far bank, following a path. Mannix and his daughter lived over here, supposedly off-limits to the timber beasts on the other shore. He ascended a hill, and then, from within the cut timber, saw the light shining in the cabin window.

He took out a cigarette, shielded it with his hand in a special way he knew, and lit it. He watched the cabin. He watched it too hard; or maybe the wind was wrong. He should have smelled her perfume before she came up behind him.

"Fargo," she whispered.

He jumped and turned. Barbara was

there on the path. She still wore the tight shirt and jeans but now the shirt was open to her waistband and he saw the double pothooks that were the shadow-outlined lower slopes of her breasts.

His gray eyes narrowed under white brows. "What are you doin' out here at this time of night?"

She laughed softly, a sound from deep in her chest. "It's only nine-thirty. Is that late?"

"In a lumber camp."

She came up to him, put a small hand on his wrist. "I haven't lived in a lumber camp all my life."

"I gathered that," said Fargo dryly.

She put a quick finger to her lips. "Shhh. My — father has the most fantastic ears." Her other hand clamped on his. "Don't talk," she whispered. "Not yet." Then she pulled him and he followed, partly curious, partly aroused by her touch.

She led him down into a kind of hollow where small fir formed an impenetrable barrier all around. It was like a fragrant bedroom. She sank to the ground, lay back against the needles. She had never let go of his wrist and now she pulled him down beside her. "Fargo," she said, "you know, it's a hell of a lonely life to be the only girl in a camp full of men."

If there had been light in this dark place it would have gleamed on teeth revealed in a wolf's smile. "I'd think it'd be a hell of an interestin' life for a girl."

"Not with my — not with Lance Mannix. He watches me all the time, like a hawk."

"He ain't watchin' you now."

She laughed softly, huskily. "That's because he killed half a bottle of booze before he went to bed."

"The Forest Service don't usually hire drunks."

"They hired him," Barbara's laugh was bitter. "Before Wilson was elected, he was President Taft's second cousin. By the time the Democrats came in, he was already entrenched. They didn't bother with small potatoes like him."

"You aren't crazy about your old man," Fargo said.

"My old man. No. I've lived with him too long. I don't have much respect left for him. He's a drunk, and he's weak. I like strong men." Her hand tightened on his; her face was close to his, her lips . . . "You understand Fargo? Strong men." Then she moved his hand, and when it came to rest he knew what she wanted.

He pushed his hand down hard against all that softness. She moaned, and then he felt her lips on his. They stayed there for a long time. When she broke away she moaned, "Oh, Fargo . . . "

There was a rustling in the darkness. She was pushing down all that tight denim. His groping hand touched smooth, naked flesh; her mouth came up to seek his again. Fargo moved. He let her hand unlatch his belt.

He had his own knot to unwind,

119

after climbing that damned tree four times that afternoon. For a while, in her receptive embrace, he let it go.

Then it was finished. She lay beside him, cradled on his arm, hand stroking the hard muscles. "Oh, Fargo. Oh, oh . . . "

He came back to rationality. "Fargo," she whispered, "every night, you hear? Every night."

"Yeah, if I can. But your Dad . . . "

"He'll drink himself to sleep. Like he always does . . . " Her voice was drowsy; her lips played over his hard chest where she had unbuttoned his shirt. "He'll never know Fargo, come back tomorrow night. Here."

"Maybe," Fargo said. "Maybe not."

She tensed beneath him. "What do you mean, maybe not?"

"They say you're bad luck. A Jonah."

"Who says that?"

"A lot of people; Duke for one."

She laughed. "Duke — that big puppy dog. Fargo, please . . . " Her nails dug into his back.

120

He pulled away, arose, put his clothes together. "All right," he said. "Tomorrow, if I can." He tucked the Batangas knife into its seat in his hip pocket. "I've got to go now."

"But — yes. Tomorrow."

"We'll see." He turned away, climbed out of the hollow. Pausing, he heard the rustle of her footsteps going to the cabin. He lit a cigarette. Oh, yes, by damn. It was phony. It was phony as a nine-dollar bill. She and her father and . . . It stank. The whole set-up that brought a woman into a logging camp — something unprecedented — stank.

He walked through the woods, came to the dam. He descended the bank, walked out, jumped the spillway, landed surefootedly, caulked soles digging in. Straightened out, went on. Then halted.

Here the river was fifty yards wide. He had traversed half that distance. How he knew that someone else was on the dam he could not say. But he sensed a presence in the darkness ahead of him.

The pistol was under his mackinaw, but that was not what he reached for. His hand fished the Batangas knife from its sheath, his wrist flicked, and both handles peeled back to lock within his hard palm, leaving ten inches of fantastically hard and sharp steel exposed. Then Fargo moved on, carefully.

His movement and that of who else was here was masked in the rushing sound of water pouring down the spillway. Fargo kept the knife pointed outward, low, parallel to the dam, in a knife-fighter's stance. Then he saw the blackness that until now he had only sensed. It loomed ahead of him on the dam.

It moved then, and he saw, too, the ax-blade limned against the sky, coming down in a sharp, chopping motion.

It was wielded expertly. If he had not had superlative reflexes that swishing stroke would have decapitated him. But the double-bitted blade went by over his ducking head, and then Fargo charged in before the blade could come back again. He thrust out with the knife.

When you cut a man in the belly with a knife you can feel the two distinct phases of your killing. First the resistance as the blade penetrates the taut web of muscle; then the easy, soft part, when it lands home in the viscera. Fargo felt both now in his knife hand which seemed, for the moment, to have a life and sensibility of its own. He heard the man on the dam grunt, gag. He heard the ax drop, splashing, into the river. He twisted the knife. When he jerked it upwards the man tried to scream but it was cut off short, to a moaning gurgle. Then the body pulled away from the blade; there was another splash as it fell into the Wolf's Head River.

Fargo crouched there, knife at the ready, for another instant. Then he ran across the dam, up the bank. He ran through the sleeping camp and, totally soundlessly, entered the bunkhouse. The chorus of snores still rang within it.

Fargo chucked his clothes, rolled into his bunk. He had sheathed the knife now, but his Colt .38 was at the ready under his Hudson's Bay five-point blanket. He lay awake for a long time, waiting to see if anyone else in the bunkhouse was awake. When he was convinced that no one was, he slowly relaxed and went to sleep.

6

DUKE assembled the crew early the next morning. A towering, massive figure with hands rammed into the pockets of stagged pants, thick legs widespread, he bellowed, "All right, dammit! We're missin' a man! Fella named Sam Goodis, bucker on Side Three — that new fella I hired jest before we pulled outa Seattle. He's gone and so's an ax! Anybody seen Goodis?"

The men were silent, shrugging. Fargo thought, *that's who he was.* Another of Lasher's men planted in the crew . . . The death of Hoskins should have stopped the opening of the new Side for days, cost MacKenzie time and timber. Fargo had unexpectedly filled the gap and so he'd had to be gotten rid of, too. Instinctively, his hand went to the .38, harnessed under his armpit inside the flannel shirt. How many more of Lasher's people were there here? Damn it, he wished he could carry the shotgun —

They searched the area. Below the dam, the Wolf's Head was wild, brawling; there was no sign of the body or the ax. Finally Duke gave up in disgust. "Hell, the work was too much for him. One of these damn hot-stove loggers; he musta high-tailed it out last night, ashamed to face me. All right, let's get back to work!"

They moved out into the virgin timber. With no need at the moment for a high-climber or rigger, Fargo was paired with Milligan at falling. They began to cut the Douglas fir. Like everything else in high-lead logging, it was an art — dropping each huge tree in exactly the right direction and on the perfect spot to make it easy for the buckers to cut it into shorter lengths, the choker setters to fix the collars, the leverman on the yarder to bring the great sticks of fir rampaging through the woods on end, like charging, maddened beasts. First the undercut in the standing trunk — and it has to be placed exactly, governing the direction of the fall. That was an art, taking into consideration the lean of the tree, the prevailing wind, everything that might affect the way one of the giants might fall. Fargo and Milligan, on either side, swung axes in rhythm, never missing a beat, huge, bright, fragrant chips flying. Then the crosscut saw was used, with wedges driven to keep it from binding, kerosene on the blade to dissolve the glue-like pitch, the blood of trees. When the cut was nearly done they could feel it in the saw handles, a kind of vibration. Looking up, they could see the treetop, scores of yards above them, began to whip. The saw withdrawn, they jumped back, and the old cry rang out, "Timberrrr — !" The tree lurched forward, there was a rending sound as the rest of the wood in its thick butt went. Slowly, majestically, the tall firs toppled until the butt broke free, kicked up and out with terrible power. Then, with terrific speed and force tons of wood came hurtling down, striking with a crash like thunder in a shower of dirt and branches. The bucklers attacked it like ants swarming on a carcass, axes flying as they lopped off limbs, and Fargo and Milligan moved on to their next victim.

It was man's work, and even though Fargo's muscles, not yet adjusted, still ached a bit when the quitting whistle blew, he felt good, relaxed, easy. After the meal, he eased out of camp without being missed, faded into the woods, loped up the river bank silently and stealthily as a shadow. He craved a swim, wanted to wash away the day's sweat and pitch — and then he had something else in mind.

A long way up the river he found a place secret enough. After what had happened last night — the fight on the dam — he had no intention of making himself vulnerable by stripping off clothes and rendering himself gunless where any other assassin could make a try at him while he was unarmed. Only when he was sure he was alone and safe did he strip, pile clothes on the bank, plunge into the icy water. Even then, he never was far from the Colt which he hung close to the surface on a projecting branch.

He climbed out, dried, teeth chattering, dressed quickly. He was on the far bank from the camp now, and there was still plenty of daylight, time enough to accomplish what he intended. He checked the Colt, made sure it was loose in the holster, opened the Batangas knife with a quick flip to make sure its handles were loose and easy-moving, made a pass or two to limber his wrist with the ten-inch blade, sheathed the weapon again, and moved back into the woods.

Despite all the mist and fog of the mornings, they were dry. This was the tag end of summer, the beginning of fall, the fire season. The needles under his feet were brittle and if he had stepped on twig or branch it would have cracked like a pistol shot. But he did not; he was like fog himself as he sifted through the shadows beneath the towering trees.

Presently he reached it; the clearing in which the Mannix cabin sat. Taking cover behind a screen of greenery, he drew from his pocket a small telescope. Opened, it was not more than a foot long but it gave him the magnification he needed. Shielding its lens with a palm lest any light from the setting sun strike it with a telltale gleam, he brought it to bear on a cabin window.

Inside, a lamp had been lit. Presently Barbara Mannix moved into view. She wore the tight shirt, blue jeans. He watched her go to a cabinet, take down a bottle and a tin cup. She poured a sizeable jolt from the bottle into the cup, drank it quickly, like a man. Then, assuming herself sufficiently screened by the woods around her, she unbuttoned the shirt, stripped it off. In a moment, she was naked to the waist. She turned to the window, almost as if deliberately giving Fargo a view of those magnificent breasts. Then she evidently removed the jeans, though he could not, at the moment, see beneath the still of the window.

After that, she vanished. When she returned she wore a robe belted about her waist with a cord. She had another drink, this time straight from the bottle, and then she shifted in and out of his sight in a regular pattern; evidently she was cooking supper.

There was no sign of her father, and there was only one horse in the little pen behind the house. The light began to fade. Then Fargo's keenly tuned hearing caught the sound of hoofbeats. Approaching from the direction of the logging camp, Lance Mannix rode into the clearing.

Fargo hunkered down a little more tightly behind his cover. He watched Mannix swing down, tilt back the

Forest Service hat, and the telescope picked up the man's face in profile as he began to unsaddle the horse. He was, Fargo thought, a damn hard-looking customer, and he handled the heavy stock saddle as if it were a feather; there was strength aplenty in those wide shoulders and thick arms, despite the marks of heavy drinking on his countenance and the beginning of a whiskey-belly under his belt. He turned the horse into the corral, put up the bars, then strode into the cabin.

Fargo swung the scope back to the window. Mannix went straight to the cabinet, got out the bottle, pulled its cork with his teeth, and drank directly from it, long and deeply. He shuddered slightly, then drank again. He and Barbara traded a few words. Apparently she was asking him if he wanted food; and, it seemed, he'd rather drink. The two of them were framed directly in the window and, right now, Fargo wished that the ability to read lips were among his skills.

But it was clear that their words were growing heated. He saw Barbara's lips peel back in a kind of snarl, the face of Mannix darken as the argument built up. He saw the Government man's big hand clench; now Barbara was yelling at him. Suddenly Mannix hit her, fast and hard, with open palm. The blow knocked her out of Fargo's vision, but she bounced back quickly. And now — Fargo tensed — she had a table knife in her hand. She came at her father with it, and the big man dodged the thrust with surprising speed. And it was, Fargo realized, a thrust that was meant to kill!

Then he caught her wrist, twisted. The knife fell to the floor, Barbara squirmed, struck at him with clawed hand, the robe flying open, big breasts bouncing. Mannix hit her again. Suddenly she quit fighting. He said something fiercely to her; she stared back at him with lambent eyes, lips parted. All at once her shoulders slumped, her face changed. Mannix grinned coldly.

Then, as Fargo watched, he pulled her to him. She came willingly. Mannix's hand went inside the open robe, closed over one breast. He bent his head, Barbara raised hers, and Fargo saw how her lips were parted. He swore softly as Mannix kissed her long and hard and in a way far from fatherly. And when the kiss was over and Mannix let her go, she snuggled against him tightly, easily, her hands under his coat, caressing his torso. He bent his head to kiss her again; then they moved out of the range of Fargo's vision, Barbara's arms around his neck.

Fargo lay there for a long time but they did not reappear.

His gray eyes were cold, hard, thoughtful, when at last, he got to his feet and faded into the woods, darkening with oncoming night. Father and daughter? Not damned likely. He had seen too many times the same sort of fight and reconciliation between whores and their fancy men. That couple in there was a young girl and a desperately jealous, hard-drinking older lover. They could not bear to be separated, and that was why Mannix had brought her out here and passed her off as his daughter.

And so, he had lied. In how many other ways had he lied?

Fargo was like a ghost as he loped downriver. When he reached the dam he faded into the underbrush, scrutinized it in the dying light to make sure the coast was clear. Then he crossed the Wolf's Head on it, sauntered on into camp. But, almost immediately, he halted, cocking his head. On the main road in from outside, wagons were coming — a lot of wagons. And that was strange, since no supplies were needed now.

He sauntered casually to one side of the clearing. Others had heard the sound, too, and the loggers had come out of their bunkhouses. Milligan came up to him. "Hey, Fargo, where you been? I thought you and me might have a game of cribbage."

"I went to take a swim," said Fargo. "Who's coming in?"

"Damned if I know." Then Milligan stiffened as, at the head of a cavalcade, a buggy appeared. The Irishman pointed.

"Hey, look. Ain't that The Old Man hisself? Ain't that Alec MacKenzie?"

It was, and the owner of Great Northwestern was in woods clothes, flannel shirt, stagged pants and caulked boots, when he got out of the vehicle. But that was not what arrested Fargo's attention.

It was the two wagonloads of men behind MacKenzie that pulled into the camp. Some of them — and there were more than two dozen — were in woods clothes, too, but they were not loggers. Fargo had seen too many of their kind to be deceived. And the rifles they carried cinched it. These were fighting men.

Fargo's nostrils flared. What Milligan had scented was like a distant crown fire. What Fargo smelled now — an old, familiar taint — was war.

* * *

Duke Hotchkiss had emerged from the office. He was obviously startled to see his boss, and even more amazed at the two wagonloads of men. Fargo could not hear the conversation that took place between the bull of the woods and the company president there outside the small log building, but he saw Duke wave his hands, frown, then shrug. Then MacKenzie turned, looked around, and his eyes came to rest on Fargo. He pointed, "You," he said. "Come here."

Fargo's mouth twisted. It was war, all right. He strode over. "Hello, Mr. MacKenzie."

"Fargo, I'd like to talk to you, along with Duke. Inside."

"Sure," Fargo followed the two of them into the office. MacKenzie shut and latched the door behind them.

He took Duke's chair behind the desk, motioned to two other chairs. Duke's eyes went from MacKenzie to Fargo with puzzlement. "You two know each other?"

"We know each other," MacKenzie said. "I hired Fargo."

"The hell you did? I hired him, after a fight — " Then Duke broke off. "Oh," he said with comprehension. "Undercover man."

"That's right," the tall Scot said. "But he's not going to be undercover anymore. He's going to have the chance to do what he hired out to — fight."

"Look, Mr. MacKenzie, maybe you'd better explain this." Duke rubbed his face. "We jest get back into the woods with a full ticket and here you show up with two dozen more men we don't need, all armed to the teeth — "

"I'll explain it," MacKenzie said. "And we need the men." He took out a cigar, bit off its end, thrust it between his teeth. "From now on, I'm taking personal charge of this operation."

Duke's leathery face registered surprise; his eyes widened, his jaw dropped. "I ain't been runnin' it to suit you?"

"You're running it all right, even if you did lose Hoskins yesterday."

"I told you, that was an accident; he cut his own climbin' rope."

"Maybe." MacKenzie arose, began to pace the office. "Be that as it may, we've got to do two things from now on — cut timber and fight. Duke, you'll handle the logging. But the fighting's Fargo's responsibility from now on — that's his speciality."

Duke rubbed his chin. "It sure as hell is."

"Anyhow," MacKenzie continued, "right after you and your men pulled out of Seattle, I picked up word from certain sources I have there. I thought I was in bad shape if I didn't make this cut, but it seems Saul Lasher's in worse. The way he cuts, he's painted himself into a corner, nobody will lease him timber rights to anything, and he's idle, with mill contracts he's got to make, too, if he's going to survive, not be foreclosed on by the banks. He's got to have the Wolf's Head, and he's got to have it in a hurry; the banks are shoving him hard. And there's only one way he can get it."

He lit the cigar. "My lease with the Government calls for me to exercise every precaution to protect that tract. I've tried to do that. But there's one thing that can get it cancelled within twenty-four hours and put out to the next bidder — Lasher. That's if we have a fire that destroys more than a quarter of the Tract."

Fargo sat up straight. MacKenzie went on. "This is the fire season and these woods are dry as powder, will be until the rains begin in maybe two weeks. It's the crucial time, when a single dropped match or cigarette butt can burn me right out of a fortune. The Government had made it my responsibility to see there is no fire, or if there is, I put it out before it does any significant damage. If it does,

I lose my logging rights automatically and they go to Lasher."

He blew smoke. "Until now, he's nibbled at me, not wanting a fire any more than I do because, after all, the more standing timber's left the richer he'll get if he could freeze me out some other way. But, according to my information, he's reached a point of desperation now. He'd burn a quarter of the Wolf's Head, maybe risk burning half of it to get quick possession. And he's hired men — fighting men, just like those out there in those wagons."

"I'm beginning to see," Duke muttered.

"Aye, it's clear. He's going to send his men into the Tract. They'll start fires, and if we try to put them out, they'll fight us — at least until there's been enough burn to make sure my lease is cancelled. Then he gets immediate possession, rips out everything that can be sawed, and fill his contracts and get square with the banks in a hurry. The word I

141

get is that he's hired at least two dozen men, maybe twice that many, and is funneling them out here in our woods. If he gets away with it, I'm ruined myself. So we've got to do two things at once — keep on getting logs out, and hunt down Lasher's men and stop 'em from starting fires. You log, Fargo hunts, and I take overall control of both operations."

"Goddamn," said Duke. "I've never been mixed up in a deal like this before."

"Let's hope you never are again. Once a fire gets started in this country, steep as it is, we'll have hell's own time putting it out."

He turned to Fargo. "So that's your job. I've got two dozen of the meanest, toughest bastards I could find in Seattle for you to handle. They're all woods-wise, but they're gun-wise even more." He gesture. "If Lasher's men aren't out there already they will be soon, like wolves in the brush. You find them. When you do . . . Well, any trespasser on this tract is to be shot on sight, and I'll take the responsibility."

He went to a file cabinet, fished in it, brought out a map. "You'll have to study this and range well out beyond the actual limits of the Tract. They can stay outside my territory and still set a fire that the wind will bring in."

"Duke will know the winds," said Fargo. "He can tell me how they blow and where and when, and we can spot our patrols that way."

"Good. What you're going to have to do, Fargo, is think like Lasher would; if you were gonna burn us out, where would you start?"

Fargo grinned his wolf's snarl. "Right across the river."

MacKenzie blinked. "What're you talking about?"

"Mannix. The Government man."

"The hell you say!" Duke blurted.

Fargo looked at MacKenzie, "What do you know about Mannix?"

"Nothing, except that he showed up at my office in Seattle with all the proper credentials, told me he'd been assigned by the Forest Service to monitor my cutting. Why?"

"Yesterday, before Hoskins fell off the spar tree, the girl, Barbara, was playing with his rope. Oh, she was clever about it, but before she was through, she'd handled it from one end to the other." His eyes were hard. "I know high-climbers and high-climbing. A man like Hoskins wouldn't cut his own rope. Somebody else did it and did it between the time he checked it in the morning and when he went up that tree. The way she played around with it, she's the logical one. A single-edge razor blade palmed between her fingers, a little sawing while she was pretending to learn high-climbing — "

"That doesn't make sense!" Duke snapped. "With her father the Ranger on the job?"

"He ain't her father. Or if he is, he's in bad trouble." Then, tersely, he told them both what he had seen through the telescope.

Duke's jaw dropped. MacKenzie's weathered face seemed to turn to stone. "You're sure," he said heavily, after Fargo was through.

"Positive." Fargo lit a cigarette, "I'd stake anything I got that she's no more his daughter than you are. She's a girl he's living with. So he's lied about that. The chances are, he's lied about a lot of other things, too. Like, for instance, being a Ranger at all."

MacKenzie frowned. "But the Government was *supposed* to send in a Ranger. And his papers were in order — "

"They probably did send a Ranger. Likely one named Mannix. But Rangers can be killed like anybody else and their papers taken. And once out here on Wolf's Head, who's to know? If Lasher needed a control out here, somebody to boss the other men he planted in your outfit, who better than this guy? He knows everything that goes on, has freedom to move anywhere he wants to. And that girl with him — she could do things nobody else could. Like slicing

Hoskins' rope. You think he'd let a man play around with something that his life depended on?"

Duke shook his head. "I still don't believe it. How'd you get on to her?"

"Who else would have had the opportunity to cut Hoskins' rope? Last night I paid a little call on her. She — got pretty friendly in a hurry. She's got slut written all over her. On top of which, she makes damned good bait. She can toll a man off by himself, away from camp, and then he can be disposed of. That's what almost happened to me last night." And he told them about the fight on the dam.

"Hell," Duke whispered. "So that's what happened to Goodis. I might have — "

MacKenzie cut in decisively. "All right, Fargo. If what you say is true, and I've no reason to doubt you, we'll take Mannix and the girl right away. We can lock them up here and keep them in custody until I can check him out with the Forest Service. Even if he is a real Ranger, we don't want him on this job." He turned to Duke. "Get some men together."

"No," said Fargo.

"What do you mean, no?"

"Let's keep the men out of this. We don't know how many of Lasher's spies are still among 'em, but once we get our hands on Mannix, we can sure as hell find out. Let's you and me and Duke take Mannix and the girl; the three of us can do it easy, come the middle of the night when everybody else is asleep. That'll leave us time to squeeze the identity of any of Lasher's men out of 'em before daybreak and take those men cold."

"Of course. You're right." MacKenzie nodded. "Okay, damn them. When I get my hands on them — " His big fists clenched. "But what if Mannix won't talk?"

Fargo's grin was not pleasant. "Leave it to me," he said. "He'll talk."

7

BY eleven o'clock the camp was sound asleep, its bunkhouses crammed with the new men. Fargo had looked them over more closely, and MacKenzie had chosen well. Seldom had he seen a tougher bunch assembled in one place. If they were loyal, God help any of Lasher's men who bumped into them!

He felt a surge of pleasure. He was glad of this development. He'd been prepared to tough it out as a logger and he didn't mind the work. But fighting was his real business, it was what he lived for, and he would be glad, he thought, to be able to sling the shotgun and wear it openly, work at the trade he loved.

Meanwhile, he had turned in with the rest of the outfit, lest his absence arouse suspicion. Now, like a great cat, he rolled out of the bunk, stood listening. All around him the chorus of snores was loud and steady. He slipped on his mackinaw, the Colt in place beneath it. Clamping the cavalry hat at its usual hell-for-leather angle, he picked up his boots, went soft-footed out of the bunkhouse. In shadow he donned the boots, laced them tightly; then he headed for the dam.

He had almost reached it when a tick of sound startled him; he whirled the gun out in a fantastic, reflexive draw. Then MacKenzie's voice whispered, "Fargo, over here."

They waited in the shadow of a clump of saplings. Fargo joined them, holstering the Colt. He stared at Duke. "What the hell's that for?"

Hotchkiss raised the double-bitted ax. "I ain't no gunman, but God help the man gits within range of this!"

Fargo's voice was thin. "Listen, we want Mannix and the girl alive and in condition to talk."

149

"Don't worry, this is jest for self-defense."

"Likely Mannix is dead drunk anyway. All right, come on." He led them across the dam. They reached the other side and struck the path that led to the cabin in the clearing. Fargo went ahead, gun out, totally alert. He didn't anticipate trouble but he had lived to his present age by not taking anything for granted. Trouble was what you got by assuming you weren't going to have any.

Nothing untoward happened, though, and they came to the clearing's edge and halted. The cabin was dark. Fargo checked the breeze, not wanting the horses in the corral to catch their scent, spook, alarm Mannix and the girl. It was all right. He moved out into the open, crouched low, ran soundlessly to the only door the cabin had. By prearrangement, Duke took the window on one side, MacKenzie the one on the other.

Fargo had seen the heavy wooded bolt on the door, knew it would be

150

shot. Mannix would not want to take the chance of anyone's walking in on him while he was making love to the girl supposed to be his daughter. He reversed the pistol hammered on the door with its butt. "Hey, Mannix! Mannix, wake up! Fire! Fire in the woods!"

For a moment no sound answered him. Then he heard a grunt. "What? What's that?"

"Fire! Duke says to come on! We need everybody!"

"Hell — " Mannix's voice was thick, slurred. Fargo heard his footsteps; the bolt slid open. Then the door cracked. "What — ?" Mannix began again. Fargo rammed the Colt through, slammed his weight against the door. Mannix tried to throw it shut when he felt the gun's cold steel in his belly but Fargo forced it open, pushed Mannix back into the room, followed him.

"Don't move," he whispered. "You do, I'll blow you wide open!" Then he called softly. "All right, Duke! MacKenzie!"

Barbara came awake, then let out a muffled cry. "What — ?"

"Hush," Fargo said. "You make a yip, I'll kill your lover man. You stay right still, exactly where you are." Then Hotchkiss and the Scot had come in behind him. "Find a lamp," Fargo ordered. MacKenzie struck a match; an instant more and a wick caught, flooded the room with yellow light.

Mannix's face was beardy, gummy, his eyes bloodshot. He wore only the bottom half of a pair of longjohns. Behind him, in the same bed that he'd just vacated, Barbara cowered wide-eyed, pulling the sheet up over her naked body. "Fargo," she breathed. Then she stared at MacKenzie and Hotchkiss, and the ax with its blades gleaming in the lamp glow.

Mannix blinked. "Duke, what the hell is all this about?"

Before Hotchkiss could answer, MacKenzie said thinly, "You and your daughter always sleep together, Mannix?" Then anger took him. "You damned spy," he rasped, clubbing a fist. "What the hell's your real name?"

For an instant, as the words sank in, Fargo thought Mannix would try to fight. Instead, a kind of shudder rippled over the man and his shoulders slumped. "So you found out, huh?" he muttered. He dropped heavily into a chair by the table, rubbed his eyes.

"It's the truth, then? Who are you, anyway?" MacKenzie towered over him.

The man who called himself Mannix drew in a long breath. "My name's Roy Morse. She — " He jerked a thumb. "Barbara Daniels."

"And you work for Lasher?"

Morse rubbed his eyes, seemingly trying to gather his wits. "Yeah, I work for Lasher. I useta be his woods boss out in Michigan. He sent me a telegram, told me he had a job for me. I came. He gimme the papers and outfit of a Ranger named Mannix — "

"Where's Mannix?" Fargo cut in.

"Dead, where you think? Lasher told me he killed Mannix, cut him open, stuffed his corpse with rocks, then sank it in the bottom of Puget Sound. Nobody'll ever find it . . . Mannix was supposed to come here, supervise the cuttin'. I came in his place. Picked her up on the way, in a honky-tonk, she was bein' floated out of Boise, Idaho, by the town law. Brought her here with me and — "

"Okay," Fargo said. "How many more men has Lasher got planted here and who are they?"

Morse blinked "What?"

Fargo moved the gun closer to his face. "You heard me. I want to know who the spies are Lasher's planted in our camp."

"There ain't any. Not since Goodis disappeared." But Fargo read the lie in the way his eyes shifted.

Fargo laughed softly. "All right, Morse, you want to play your way, I'll play mine." He swapped the gun to his left hand; his right blurred and then the Batangas knife was in it, its point between Morse's eyes. "You've got exactly one minute to start givin' us some straight talk. Otherwise, I'll show you a few tricks with cold steel I picked up down in Mexico. You know what the Yaqui Injuns do to a man? First they cut off his eyelids — "

"For Christ's sake — " Morse's face paled. "All right, I'll talk, damn it!" His eyes shuttled to Duke, standing there with poised ax-blade, also threatening him. He pulled his face back from the point of the knife. "I'll tell you everything — " Then, in a sweeping motion, he knocked the lamp off the table and toppled the chair backwards and the room was in darkness.

"Hold it!" Fargo bellowed, after him with the knife in that same split second. "I'll take him!" He heard Morse scrambling to his feet, got his arm. "I've got — " But then Morse screamed. It was a short, sharp cry, quickly cut off; and it did not quite smother the curious *chunk* that was like a butcher cutting meat with a cleaver. Fargo felt the arm in his grasp go limp; Morse's body fell back before it had arisen.

"Goddman it," Fargo said bitterly. "Duke — "

MacKenzie had already struck a match. When it flared, the girl on the bed cried out at the sight of Morse, lying on his back, wide eyes staring sightless at the roofpoles, one blade of the double-bitted ax buried in his chest, splitting his torso wide.

Fargo whirled on Hotchkiss. "Blast it, I told you I had him! Now — " Disgustedly, he lit another lamp.

Duke shook his head. "Hell, I'm sorry. It was all so quick. All I know is that when he started to go, I swung at him. It was all so quick." He turned to MacKenzie.

The Scot nodded grimly, a gun in his own hand. "I know, Duke, I almost shot him myself when he slugged that lamp; held my fire just in time. Well . . . " He looked down at the body, grimaced. "What's done is done. We've still got her." He pointed at the girl.

"I don't know anything, so help me I don't!" Her voice trembled. "Except about Goodis and Milligan — "

Fargo stiffened. "*Milligan?*"

She nodded mutely. Her eyes went again to Morse's body, then she turned her head to the wall, the sheet clutched about her breasts.

"They were the only two I ever heard him mention," she said dully. "They were — "

The crash of glass drowned her words. The panes of a window fell in. Fargo whirled just in time to see the barrel of a .45 Colt Peacemaker rammed through. Then the gun roared. The impact of the slug caught the girl between her naked shoulder blades, threw her against the log wall beside the bed. Before the sound of the gun had died, Fargo punched a shot through the window, then another.

And knew he'd missed; the man had ducked below the sill. Fargo swept the second lamp off the table with a quick gesture, hurtled through the door. As he crossed the threshhold he threw himself sideways against the wall, taking cover in the shadows there.

That saved his life. From around the corner of the cabin, a long spurt of orange tongued at him; the .45 roared almost in his ear. The bullet cut air where he'd have been if he hadn't swerved. Fargo fired back but his own bullet chunked into the corner logs behind which the gunman dodged. Fargo eased forward, then he heard the thud of running feet. The killer was making a break across the clearing, heading for the woods.

Fargo leaped around the cabin's corner, strained to pierce the darkness. He thought he saw a tatter of movement near the edge of the woods. Then brush crashed. Fargo bellowed, "Milligan!"

At the same instant, he fell forward. As he had hoped, the killer fired once more, at the sound. The slug snarled overhead. Fargo caught the telltale muzzle-flame and fired three times, one directly on it, once to the right, then to the left. And, in the brush beyond the clearing, a man screamed.

Fargo fired again; the scream died. Then, carefully, he got to his feet. Nothing happened, and he ran forward. He probed in brush, then his booted foot kicked something solid yet yielding. He knew what it was before he bent, groped, and came up with a hand smeared with warm wetness.

Fargo let out a terse obscenity, found a match and snapped it with his thumb. In its light, the glazed eyes of Jerry Milligan glittered back like a pair of marbles. One of the hollowpoints had caught him in the chest, and he would never swing an ax again.

Or, Fargo thought, betray the man who paid his wages.

Fargo stood there looking down at the body of the man he'd worked alongside. Of course, Milligan could have spotted him when he'd left the bunkhouse, their beds were next to each other. And Milligan, sensing something wrong, could have trailed him — and then put a bullet into Barbara in a desperate attempt to keep her from giving him away. But, of course, a shade too late . . . That could have been how it happened, exactly how it happened, maybe it was.

Only, Fargo did not think so. There was something here he could not yet fit together. He lifted his head, sniffed the air. Milligan . . . He'd talked of that distant, invisible crown fire, the taint of danger a man could smell. That talk had been, of course, to throw Fargo off the track. And yet Milligan had been right. There was still something in the air, a stink of menace . . . And it did not entirely come from the knowledge that somewhere out there in the darkness, Lasher's men were gathering to burn them out.

Then MacKenzie and Hotchkiss came up behind him, the Scot wielding a carbide lantern he'd found in the cabin. Behind Fargo, Duke cursed. "Jerry Milligan! It was him, like she said!"

MacKenzie was shaking his head dazedly. "What a bloody night," he whispered. "What an awful, bloody night!"

"The girl's dead," Duke said. "That one bullet killed her, Fargo." Then he made a sound of satisfaction. "Well, this'll give Lasher something to think about. All his people rubbed out in one night, just like that!" He snapped his fingers. "Mannix, Goodis, Milligan — he sure as hell had us well-salted, didn't he? Maybe now, if Fargo can keep the firebugs off of us, we can get some timber out."

"Maybe," Fargo said. He suddenly felt very tired. "Let's get back to camp. We can clean this mess up in the morning."

"Sure," said Hotchkiss. "It's been a good night's work." He turned and led the way back past the darkened cabin

161

to the dam. Fargo stayed behind him, all the way to camp.

Fargo had slept only fitfully but there was work to do and he started early. By sunrise he was back in harness — literally. Now the trunk had been robbed of its contents; as Fargo lined up the gunmen MacKenzie had turned over to him and gave them orders, his torso was crisscrossed with ammunition bandoliers. The fat primers of ten-gauge shells glittered in one; rounds for the Winchester saddle-gun in the other. The sawed-off Fox hung down his back behind his right arm, on its sling. Now he had abandoned the shoulder harness and the Colt was seated in the *buscadero* holster on a cartridge belt around his waist. He was, in effect, a walking arsenal, but every weapon had its special use and was worth carrying a long time for the one crucial moment when it could do the job better than anything else.

The two dozen fighting men who he confronted were only slightly less heavier armed than he. Each had at least one pistol and a Winchester or Springfield rifle, and each carried a sheathed knife. They looked at him and listened to him with the respect of professionals who recognized a master of their trade.

"Okay," Fargo said. "I want you in groups of four. You've got maps showing the sectors you're to patrol. Each group of four sets up a base camp, in good cover. Two men ride the line on the day shift, while the other two sleep, then you swap over; a twenty-four-hour watch on every sector. No fires; you eat the canned grub you've been issued. If you smoke make damned sure you put out matches and cigarettes completely and totally. We're here to keep these woods from burning down, not to do the trick ourselves by accident. You run across anybody out there, shoot first and ask questions later. You spot a fire, get three men on it, the fourth signals with three shots, pauses, three more, and rides like hell for camp, here. We'll all pile in to help you. And — You're being paid good wages, but MacKenzie's offerin' a bonus. Two hundred dollars a head, for every one of Lasher's men you bring in! Any questions?"

There were none; this was only the tail-end of a thorough briefing. Fargo nodded. "All right. Mount up. And when you're on patrol, that pack mule goes where you go."

They nodded, swung into the saddles of the riding mules MacKenzie had provided from his work stock and from the wagon teams. Each group of four led a pack animal, loaded with axes, long-handled shovels and back-pack water sprays: firefighting equipment to be used to halt any blaze before it could get a fair start. Fargo went to his own mule, mounted lithely, checked the seating of his Winchester in its saddle scabbard. He took the lead-rope of his own pack animal. His job was the biggest, most demanding of all — to patrol the whole perimeter, stay in contact and make sure they did their work, kept a sharp lookout. Until the routine was shaken down and he knew how well he could trust them all, how much they could be depended on, there'd be little rest for him.

But that was why he had hired out.

MacKenzie and Hotchkiss, at his stirrup, looked up at him. "Good luck, Fargo," the Scot said. His face was taut, strained from the violence of the night before. Duke added, "Give 'em hell, Fargo."

"Yeah," he said. He brought his arm up and forward in a signal to his men. "Move out!" he called and spurred the mule.

The Wolf's Head Tract was a magnificent piece of country. By the time they had reached its limits, still untouched by logging, virgin forest towered above them, huge Douglas firs hundreds of years in age, their pointed tips seeming to scrape the very sky itself, the solitude beneath their spreading branches total, a perpetual twilight, unbroken by any sound save the whisper of the wind, the occasional chatter of a squirrel. The vast forest climbed the side of mountains, carpeted deep ravines, gave way in places to sunlit high meadows where clean swift-rushing streams foamed and plunged. This was what the Northwest had been before the white man came, and Fargo felt a touch of bitterness that it must be cut and spoiled at all. The damned politicians — If The Colonel could have his way it would remain untouched. But the politicians had taken over and so its violation was inevitable. Well, at least MacKenzie would leave something of it; Lasher would rape the mountainsides bare, gouge out the valleys, turn this fine country into a desert. Or, Fargo thought with rage and disgust, burn it into wasteland . . .

It was a damned shame that MacKenzie had to hire men out of his own pocket to keep that from happening. By rights, the whole Tract should constantly be patrolled by Forest

Rangers. But the Forest Service was a victim of the politicians, too, starved for the money they spent so freely on the pork-barrel projects that would line their own pockets. It would take more Forest Rangers than there were in the whole Northwest to stand guard against Lasher. And maybe it was just as well the job was up to him, to Fargo. Rangers were good men, but their job was not to fight . . .

He dropped his men off according to the plan he had worked out from the map before turning in, and after consulting with Duke about the prevailing winds. So far they were shaping up well; he thought he could rely on them. By morning of the second day he was alone in the wilderness.

After a breakfast of canned salmon and cold brook water, he pushed the mules high up on a mountainside. There he tethered them, and from the pack mule he unlatched a canvas bag. It contained a safety belt, climbing rope and climbing spikes, the same outfit

167

used in topping and rigging a spar. With binoculars slung about his neck, he selected a towering giant of a fir and went up it quickly but carefully. High on its flank, resting on the in-driven irons, he put the binoculars to his eyes and looked off across endless miles of broken country, all thickly furred with spruce. He searched carefully, alert for any thread of smoke, any unusual movement. There was none.

Presently, satisfied, he recased the glasses. A bough scraped against his shoulder; needles fell from it. He put up a hand, touched it appraisingly. It was waxen with stored pitch and dry and brittle. Rain . . . Damn it, what was needed was a good, heavy, two-day general rain to wet down all this country; that would pull Lasher's fuse. But there was not a shred of cloud in the whole stainless blue bowl of sky.

He went down, removed the gear, mounted up and rode on. Four more times during the day he climbed, surveyed, and saw nothing of consequence. Nor did he on the next day or the next, as he made his rounds, checking the patrols. Faithfully and without complaint, they were carrying out their assignments, observing the fire prevention rules he'd laid down. And none had anything alarming to report. Fargo began to wonder if MacKenzie's information had been straight. But with every hour, the woods grew dryer, more like a tinderbox. It might be that Lasher was waiting, biding time until the exact moment when a single thrown match would be enough to explode the Wolf's Head into a great convulsion of rolling flame.

Fargo was too old a hand to be lulled into carelessness or slackness. Remorselessly, ceaselessly, he made his rounds. And he himself never smoked, much as he liked tobacco, except beside a stream, where match and cigarette butt alike could be thoroughly doused.

Then, on the morning of the fourth day, leaning out from the climbing rope, pivoted on his spikes, glasses to his eyes, he saw it.

There, miles to the south, ominous against the brightness of the sky — a thread of smoke, long, gray and tenuous, curling up from the furry shag of distant forest! Fargo cursed. At that instant he heard, from very far away, the thunder of three shots, a pause, then the rattle of three more. He cased the binoculars, and then abandoned caution as he came rocketing down the tree.

He landed lightly on his feet, unsnapped one end of the rope and whipped it from around the tree. Instinctively, then, before doing anything else, he turned to reach for the shotgun at the fir's base where he'd propped it before beginning his ascent. It was an awkward thing to carry on a climb.

"You touch that gun, Mister, and you're dead."

Fargo froze. Then they were there, drifting out of the darkness beneath the spruce like a pair of shadows. Big men, tough men, in the clothes of loggers. And both of them held Colt automatics trained squarely on him.

8

FARGO cursed soundlessly, but he did not move. They had him cold. Hampered by the climbing irons he wore, the safety belt and rope, there was not a chance of fighting back under a dead drop of the kind they had. Slowly, raising his hands, he straightened up.

The man of the left wore a red shirt and had a beard to match. He laughed. "We coulda shot you down outa there like a squirrel, but Lasher said no. He said if we caught the fella in the Army hat, to make him talk. He wants to know what happened to his people in MacKenzie's camp. He wants to know what's goin' on there and exactly how many men you got out here and where." Then he said, "Watch him close, Jake, while I shake him down."

"Right," Jake wore a blue shirt and was cleanshaven except for a blond mustache. Red Shirt came up to Fargo carefully, whisked the Colt from its holster. Fargo was helpless as the man patted him down, frisked him, took out the Batangas knife. "That seems to clean you up pretty good. We already got the rifle off your saddle." He bent and picked up the shotgun. "Damn one-man army, ain't you?" Then he jerked the muzzle of the Colt. "Back up against the tree." With the shotgun butt he pushed Fargo against the trunk. Then he seized the loose end of the climbing rope, coiled it in his hand, unsnapped it. "This'll do to tie those mitts of yours."

He tossed the shotgun aside and did it deftly, holstering his pistol and forcing Fargo to hold out his hands, wrists together while Jake kept an unblinking watch at point blank range. While he worked, he went on talking. "I reckon you seen that smoke. First fire; come a little while from now, there'll be more. Includin' one right here. Which, I reckon you know, you're gonna be right in the middle of. But if you're a good boy and tell us what we want to know, we'll put a bullet in your head and you'll die easy. If you don't talk, we'll let you burn." He took out Fargo's Batangas knife, fiddled with it, worked it open. "A man that's been hamstrung, he can't get away from fire so easy, you know, and once we put out a little coal oil and toss a match, you'll be like an ant in a furnace — " He laughed thinly, obscenely. "Crawlin' with your tendons cut, tryin' to out-crawl the flames. Have plenty of time to feel it good, then . . . " Suddenly his grin vanished. "All right, Fargo, or whatever your name is. Lemme have the information Lasher wants. Give it to me quick and save us both a lot of trouble."

Fargo sucked in a long breath. He had been half-listening, with the rest of him appraising the situation for a chance, any chance. A half-second's distraction, that would be enough. But these gunmen knew their business; they concentrated on what they were doing, their alertness as wolflike as his own. He had to play for time. He formulated words; opened his mouth to speak.

Then the gunfire came.

It was far away, in the direction of the blaze, but it came in the long crackling roll of many weapons firing all at once, a full-scale battle. Red Shirt's eyes widened and for the blink of an eye Jake's head turned and Fargo, already knowing what to do when he had his chance, brought up one long, lean leg, its boot still shod with climbing irons, and kicked sideways. Eight inches of razor-sharp steel slid between Red Shirt's ribs. Red Shirt screamed as the climbing irons slashed his vitals and Fargo hooked his leg desperately, bringing the impaled, sagging body around and to him, as in that instant Jake fired, the bullet chunked into Red Shirt's body which Fargo had pulled between them.

Fargo made a grab for Red Shirt's gun simultaneously, but now the corpse was sagging and, with his bound hands, he missed. He kicked the iron free and dived, as Jake, firing again, sent a bullet whinning past his head.

He landed hard, bound hands clamping the shotgun stock just behind the breech, rolled, and another bullet struck the woods duff where his body had been. Then, slipping the safety of the fully loaded weapon, he came up as yet another .45 slug burned a rip across his upper arm. His fingers found the double-triggers; he pointed the gun in the general direction of Jake and fired both barrels.

That was the beauty of the weapon; eighteen buckshot spraying from those open bores made a pattern nothing could escape, even if there was no time to aim. Jake was squeezing off another shot when the barrage caught him full on, picked him up and flung him backward. The bullet whined into the air. The bloody thing that had been Jake lay motionless and Fargo wasted not an instant on it, knowing in advance what that charge could do. He gained his feet, lurched in the bloody spikes to Red Shirt's sprawled carcass, found his Batangas knife. He thrust its sharp point into the fir trunk and with it fixed firmly there sawed the climbing rope off around his wrists.

As soon as he had freed his hands he crammed two more rounds into the shotgun — the first law of survival. Then he worked off the spikes, unfastened the safety belt. He found his hat — knocked free in the dive — clamped it on his head, thrust his Colt back into the holster. Fully armed again, he ran for the tethered mules. Down there to the south, all hell was breaking loose. His men must have clustered to put out the fire, and Lasher's men were trying to keep them from it.

He was on the mule's back in a flying leap, seizing the pack animal's rope. He drove in spurs, sent both mules rocketing through the woods, headed down the slope and south, and he rode with the shotgun at the ready. Lasher had made his play. There'd be more of his men scattered through the woods.

* * *

This time he saw them before they saw him. He'd gone five miles when he caught the pungent smell of smoke close by. His head swiveled like that of a beast of prey seeking the scent of quarry as he tested the wind. Then he saw its source, a small clearing just ahead, not much bigger than a room, saw a bright tongue of orange and the colors of men's clothes moving among the trees. There was no time for stealth; he slammed the mule with spurs again.

They heard him coming, turned as he broke out of the fir into the clearing. Lasher's men were also traveling in pairs; the two of them whirled, stood frozen in surprise, one with lighted match still in hand, the other about to begin the pouring of kerosene. Their eyes widened at the sight of Fargo; he was the last thing they ever saw.

He fired the shotgun on the run, right barrel, shift aim, left. One of them, caught low, had time to scream and kick; the other died outright, the kerosene can dropping from his hand. Behind the bodies, a small flame, campfire size, was growing rapidly. Fargo jerked the mules to a skidding halt. He was off his mount in a long leap, clinging to its reins as it snorted at the smell of smoke. With his other hand he fought loose one of the backpack spray canisters from the mule. He worked the plunger three, four times, frantically; then it had regained what pressure had leaked out during the morning. He locked the plunger, pointed the hose, pulled the trigger on the nozzle. Water arced, sprayed, caught the flames beginning to lick at a dry trunk, trying to climb it at the clearing's edge. Like a frightened animal trying to escape, the fire crawled back down the trunk flowed off in two directions through the duff. Fargo pulled the mules closer, hugging the spray with one hand, and fired water again; flame hissed, smoke and steam roiled up together. The bright arteries of orange winked out, leaving only glowing sparks.

Only then did Fargo tie the mules. In the distance he could still hear the popping of guns; it had increased rather than diminished. But he could not go on until this fire was out. He doused all sparks, stirred the duff, with a shovel, worked five, ten precious minutes to make sure he had caught every glowing coal. Then he reloaded spray and shovel, mounted up, rode on toward the sound of the guns, not giving the bodies in the clearing a second glance, two more rounds in the loaded sawed-off.

It was a breakneck ride, one of the roughest he'd ever taken over treacherous country. On a horse, he'd never have made it but the mules were surefooted and nimble. They skittered with agility down slopes, leaped obstructions, struggled up hillsides slippery with dry needles, never slowed for ledges that a horse would have had to walk along. But as the sound of shooting grew louder they began to shy and balk. It was not the gunfire as it was the smell that clogged their nostrils — and those of Fargo. For now the air was thick and rank with woodsmoke, and he could see it drifting grayly through the trees.

Then, from behind a log, a man reared up, directly in his path. Fargo almost fired before he recognized the char-smudged face of one of his own crew. "Davis!" he snapped. "What the hell?"

Davis dropped back behind the log. "Git down, Fargo! These damn woods are full of snipers!"

Fargo wasted no time with questions. He left the saddle in a flying leap. At that instant, his riding mule brayed, dropped, caught by a bullet behind the foreleg. Fargo snatched the Winchester free just before the creature's body smashed it. The pack mule, its leadrope tied to the dead mule's saddle horn, reared back, pawed and fought, but could not free itself. Fargo heard a bullet chunk into wood, felt splinters from the log's top in his face as he dived behind it and landed flat there next to Davis.

He levered a round into the rifle's chamber. "What's goin' on?"

"They set a big one here! It's still burnin'. We all gathered, tried to put it out. They was waitin' for us, opened up on us. We been fightin' for the whole mornin'. We used the smoke for cover, managed to control the blaze for a spell, but they brought in more men. We had to give up, it's caught good now, burnin' like hell down the valley. And we're gonna have to clean out Lasher's men before we can do anything about it!"

"All right," said Fargo grimly. "Then

we'll clean 'em out." Cautiously, he swiveled his head, trying to appraise the situation. They were in a wide ravine, thickly clad with fir on either side. "Our men are all up and down this slope, Lasher's on yonder one," Davis told him. "The fire's burnin' down the floor of the ravine, away from us, thank God. It's still on the ground. If we can clear out those birds over yonder, we might still stop it if it don't crown. But it's gittin' bigger all the time and if the wind rises, it'll crown out sure, and once it's in the treetops there'll be hell to pay!" Suddenly he raised his Springfield, fired, then dropped back. "Missed!" he growled. "Can't see a damned thing in this smoke! We sent a man into camp. One hope is that a crew'll git here from there to help us, but even so it'll be damned near night before they can — " Suddenly he fired again. "Aha, you son'bitch!" he chortled as a man screamed on the other slope. "Before they git here," he finished. "And if those bastards keep us pinned down 'til then . . . "

"They won't." Fargo had the layout locked firmly in his mind now. "Listen," he said. "You got a match with you?"

"Plenty. What — ?"

"I'm goin' down the line," said Fargo. "Pass the word to the others. When you hear this shotgun go off twice, that's the signal. You throw a match out down there in the ravine, get a fire goin'."

"Another fire?" Davis blinked, then ducked as a bullet whined overhead.

"We're gonna do that all along here." His hand gestured, to take in the length of the ravine. "The wind'll blow it right on down behind the first fire, and it'll go out when it hits where that's already burned. Meanwhile, we'll need a smoke screen. As soon as this ravine is plumb full of smoke, I'll blast the shotgun two more times. Then we charge. We'll go up that slope across there behind the smoke and come out like The Rough Riders at San Juan Hill!" He grinned his wolf's grin. "Dig those birds over yonder out like ticks!"

Comprehension dawned on Davis. "Sure, hell, yes! It'll work if the wind don't change."

"That's a chance we have to take." He did not add what both knew — that if it did, they'd fry. There was no time for wasted words. With the shotgun slung, the rifle at the ready, he came up from behind the log, ran slipping and dodging through the trees.

Bullets whined around him; taking cover behind a spruce, he fired back at a wink of gunflame on the far bank, visible in the deep woods gloom. He thought he heard a man cry out; then he ran on.

His own men, more than a dozen, were behind logs or tree trunks. Twice they nearly shot him by mistake before he identified himself. They listened keenly, intently, as he explained his plan, then nodded, grinning. They'd had enough of being pinned down. Besides, if the wind changed, the fire circled them; the flames would do what Lasher's men so far had not been able to. It was time to move, time for action.

Fargo fired the shotgun. Burning fir boughs and thrown matches sailed out and down the slope of the ravine. A dozen little fires started, instantly boiling up plumes of smoke. The wind, not strong, gently merged them. The trick, Fargo thought, was to wait until the smoke was thick enough but not to wait until the fires had grown into a barrier that would bar their way. That would take nice judgment . . . Meanwhile, each side went on shooting.

As lead whined back and forth from slope to slope, the bright flames glittered in the dry fir needles on the floor of the ravine. Like water filling a well, the gray-white smoke began to fill the hollow; it rose up each bank, wafted through the trees, acrid in the nostrils, searing in the lungs, painful in the eyes. Now the hollow was full of smoke and it made a rising, drifting wall that veiled Fargo and his men from the other side. So it was time to go . . . He looked up and down his line but his men had become invisible in the white blanket; he could hear them coughing and gagging. His lips peeled back from his teeth in his wolf's snarl, and then he thumbed two more shotgun shells from his bandolier. With these cradled in his palm, he triggered off the rounds in the Fox's chambers toward the far slope, and the double roar was the signal for the charge. Fargo crammed in the fresh rounds, closed the gun, and sprang to his feet. "Let 'em have it!" he bellowed and charged into the ravine.

His caulk-shod soles gave him sure purchase on the steep hillside. He went full tilt into that cauldron of smoke, dodging trees, the shotgun in one hand, the Winchester in the other. On the other side, Lasher's men were firing blindly, and Fargo heard the old, familiar, deadly whisper of lead passing by. At least one of the enemy's shots connected; in the bottom of the ravine, a man cried out. But on either flank Fargo's forces were with him; he could hear them cursing, grunting, and firing as they hurtled down the hill.

Then they had reached the flames. In such dry duff it was amazing how fast a fire could build, and the blazes kindled by Fargo and his men to build the smokescreen tongued higher than he had expected. Even he balked momentarily at the orange barrier, nearly waist-high, licking hungrily at the layers of fir needles on the floor of the ravine, gobbling saplings and fallen limbs. Instinctively, he recoiled from the searing blast of heat. But there was nothing for it. He bellowed, "Come on!" and plunged into the fire.

Though long and extended down the valley, the band of flames was not yet wide. Fire licked at Fargo's canvas pants, scorched and singed them, and, in places, the skin beneath them. The heavy boots protected his feet and ankles. Holding his breath, eyes closed, shotgun and rifle high, he dove through the barrier, emerged, slapping at the smoldering spots on his clothes. Then, under cover of the roiling smoke, he charged up the hill. And his men came with him, firing as they went.

It was Kettle Hill in Cuba all over again, he thought crazily, only there had been no smokescreen at Kettle Hill and the Spanish riflemen had had a clear field of fire for their Mausers. But it was an infantry charge to take the high ground against a dug-in force, and for an instant he wished The Colonel could be here; he would have enjoyed it. Then, scrambling up the slope, Fargo quit thinking and concentrated on fighting.

Suddenly, they burst from the smoke, a straggling line of gasping men with blackened faces and streaming eyes. Now they were in the big timber almost at the top, and in close combat.

Lasher's men had drawn back, upwards, to keep above the smoke. Now, at nearly point-blank range, they unleashed a hail of fire.

Lead made a sleetstorm around Fargo as he sucked in breath, blinked his watery eyes to clear them. He saw the white blur of faces, the bright tongues of muzzle-flames above him. He let out a yell of sheer excitement, half Apache war-whoop, half wolf-howl, threw the rifle aside and began to use the shotgun.

This was the work for which it had been designed. Fargo raked the slope, one-handed, his other jerking shells from the bandolier. He broke and loaded and closed and fired the gun so fast that its thundering reports seemed to merge together in one long roll. And, pivoting his body, he laid down a barrage of buckshot from left to right and back again, as, up there, dead ahead, men were flushed out of cover like startled rabbits . . . Or died where they lay, riddled by those chopping slugs known with good reason as 'blue whistlers'.

He saw one beanpole figure rise from a clump of saplings, leveling a rifle, saw it go down like a cut tree; another body plunged from underbrush head-first, went somersaulting absurdly down the slope to vanish in the smoke, wind up sprawled in the flames below. A man leaped out from behind the bole of a mighty fir just in front of him as Fargo, twisted, off-balance, fired rounds to the right. He had guts; taking advantage of the split-second when Fargo could not bring the gun to bear, he aimed carefully, at a range of no more than five yards. Fargo saw him from the corner of his eye and there was an instant when time seemed to stop. In that eye-wink, he was as close to death as he would ever come. He twisted, slung the shotgun at the man as hard as he could, blindly, and was already falling before the fellow's Colt went off, his own hand digging for his holstered pistol. A bullet ripped his ear, notching it and spraying blood, burning across his neck. Then he had fired, instinctively, across his own torso; and the thrown shotgun had bought him his life and cost that of his attacker. Hurtling through the air, it had caused the man to flinch; otherwise, his bullet would have torn Fargo's skull apart. He never fired a second one because the .38 hollowpoint drove into his solar plexus and blew apart there and he toppled backward, dead before he hit the ground. Fargo's body did not halt its whirling motion; he dived forward, scooped up the Fox from where it had fallen near the dead man, straightened and began to rake the woods again.

And now Lasher's men were falling back, their fire diminished. Fargo's little army had taken casualties, but it came on, mercilessly, inexorably, and now the fighting was hand to hand. A bearded man in a beaver-hide Stetson materialized suddenly from behind a huge log as Fargo scrambled over it. There was no room for gunplay; he seized Fargo, jerked him around, got one hand on Fargo's throat, closed it savagely. Fargo brought up the shotgun butt with all his strength. It caught the bearded man under the chin, snapped his mouth shut with a crunch that meant a broken jaw. The man howled thickly, sagged; his hand slid loose from Fargo's throat as he dropped. Fargo drove the shotgun butt between his eyes. Then he ran on, not even pausing to administer a killing shot. It would have been superfluous, he had felt bone give under the second blow. He whirled, though, as someone else came at him from the flank, and just in time he held his fire. It was Davis, white teeth shining in a soot-blackened face. "They're breakin'!" Davis yelled. "They're on the run! We've won!"

"Wipe 'em out!" Fargo yelled in reply. "Clean 'em up! No quarter, no survivors! And do it in a hurry! We've got to fight that fire!" He ran on through the woods, looking for a target. Around him men struggled, wrestled; he saw a knife blade rise and fall. A gun went off, then another; and then all shooting died. Suddenly the woods were still save for the distant crackling of the fire, a frightened mule braying somewhere across the ravine. The fight was over. Bodies lay among the trees like fallen fruit from an overripe orchard, scattered everywhere. One wounded man tried to rise; Fargo saw Davis line a pistol, pull the trigger, the man fell back. Davis turned to Fargo, half sick, half defiant. "Damn it," he rasped, "he had it coming! Any man that'd try to burn the woods — "

Only men who lived in the big timber and who had fought forest fires and seen their fellows burned alive and whole settlements wiped out and wild game turned to charred obscenities could understand the hatred of the arsonists that glittered in Davis' eyes.

Fargo nodded. "Right," he snapped. "Now, let's see to our own wounded and tackle that damn fire before it crowns!"

★ ★ ★

Lasher's firebugs had started flames along a front of nearly a hundred yards hours before, and then had battled the MacKenzie crew to keep them from dealing with it. Now, across and beyond the ravine, the fire had spread greedily, hungrily, for a mile or more, gathering intensity with every wasted minute. The fir needles, accumulated over ages in deep, pitch-filled layers, burned like wax; flames roared between the tree trunks higher than a man's head, and beneath the pressure of the wind which, fortunately, had not risen, leaped westward, roughly in the direction of the lumber camp miles away. The fight had taken place upwind, behind the fire, and the smokescreen blazes Fargo set had spread only until they reached the area already burned; then, for lack of fuel, they went out. But the original conflagration surged onward, remorselessly, though by a miracle it had not crowned, and there was still a chance of checking it.

The battle had cost Fargo three men

killed and two badly wounded of his original dozen. He loaded the wounded men on mules, and sent a man with a lesser wound to oversee them as they started for the lumber camp in a roundabout way that should keep them clear of flames unless the wind changed. That left, counting himself, only seven, but reinforcements were now drifting in as the remainder of his patrols, in pairs or quartets, left their posts and rode for the smoke. By the time — leading their fractious mules — they had circled the fire and come out downwind, ahead of it, in a ghastly blast of heat and sparks, his crew had swollen to fifteen.

Fargo took a moment to appraise the situation. Two hundred yards away the flames were a bright orange wall amidst the vast old trees, and coming closer at the gait of a walking man. To the uninitiated eye it was already a fearsome sight but he and every man with him knew how much worse it could be.

Fire moved in two ways: on the ground and in the treetops. As long as it was only on the ground it could be checked; there was at least a chance. Fire lanes could be cleared and backfires set, carefully controlled, to burn ahead and toward it and rob it of its fuel. But once it ceased to walk and started to climb and fly, that was a very different matter.

So far the fact that this was virgin timber had kept the fire grounded. The trees here had shaded out all smaller growth, their own trunks soaring sixty, seventy, a hundred feet upward before the first branches began. The flames gnawed around their bases, climbed their trunks, but could not as yet reach their branches; even the sparks went out before they had swirled high enough to set fire to the treetops. But that was all by grace of wind. Let the breeze from the mountains rise a few more knots to fan the flames and then the firc would crown. Windblown embers lodging in the branches would burst the treetops into flame and the blaze would travel overhead, out of reach, in a vast inferno, like an army of demonic apes swinging from limb to limb. When that happened, its speed would exceed that of the fastest horse, its heat create a storm, and it could leap behind the firefighters in a flash, encircle them, trap them and incinerate them. A crown fire was deadly, swift, merciless, the worst enemy of the woodsman and the logger.

Calmly contemplating this, Fargo lit a cigarette, although his throat and lungs were already seared with woodsmoke. He stood there with his men around him for a full minute, quietly, watching the flames come on. What he was doing was, within his head, reconstructing the maps of this territory, of the Wolf's Head Tract that he had studied every day since putting out his patrols. Then he made his decision.

He turned to his men. "Get your mules and pack animals and mount up and follow me."

Much as it galled him, he had to yield square miles to the flames, sacrifice irreplaceable acreage of virgin timber to save the rest. But with the few men he had, he could not stop the fire here, that was hopeless. He had to fall back to a stronger position.

In his mind, as he swung into the saddle, he saw the country as if he were a circling hawk looking down at it from high in the air. He saw its streams and mountain meadows, and he pieced them together in a line of defense, with a route for retreat if necessary. To the north, the Wolf's Head River poured down out of the hills, and it would form a sort of barrier that might check the fire in that direction. He had to worry about the west, toward which the east wind was driving the flames.

Ten miles away in that quarter of the compass another stream called Snow Fork ran from south to north to join the Wolf's Head. It was not nearly wide enough to suit him but it was a natural fire lane of sorts, a barrier to the flames. That was where they would begin the battle. If they rode fast enough they might buy time enough to get a band of forest cleared to form a gap that the flames could not leap. It would put them closer, too, to the reinforcements from the lumber camp which, ultimately, they had to have to win. And, most important, the wind would come from a different angle there, driving eastward toward the flames, allowing them to set a backfire. He had fed all those factors through the machinery of his mind in the length of time it took to smoke the cigarette and grind its butt out thoroughly and hit the saddle.

Then they rode, hard and fast.

9

THERE was nothing glamorous about fighting a forest fire. It was damned hard, grinding, dangerous work with ax and shovel and crosscut saw. They reached the stream, Snow Fork, and Fargo's heart sank as he saw how narrow it was in actuality and how close the woods grew on either bank. He had hoped for open, rocky country around the Fork, but that was not to be.

He wasted no time in recrimination or disappointment. Instead, he had the mules taken to the far bank, tethered there, and he and his crew fell to work like madmen. What they had to do was cut timber and gouge out duff, clear as wide and long a fire lane as they could before the flames got here. It was, of course, impossible for so small a crew to build a complete barrier to the fire, but more men from the camp would be here soon and any progress they made meanwhile might swing the balance in the long run. if they could stop the fire here it would have consumed many acres, but still far from the crucial quarter of the Wolf's Head that would get MacKenzie's lease cancelled overnight.

So, tired, sooty and bullet-marked as they were, they pitched in. Experienced woodsmen all, they wasted not a stroke of ax nor swing of saw. Huge trees that had stood for centuries, toppled before their onslaught in a time incredibly short. After all, they had not need to fell them in any particular direction. Like termites they ate a hole in the woods up and down the river, dropping timber, shoveling duff. They put the mules to work, too, with improvised drags that scraped away the inflammable mound of the forest floor to bare earth.

Best of all, Fargo thought, the wind was right. As soon as they had a safety notch cleared, they could set a backfire. The wind, hurtling down from the mountains in a different quarter, would drive it like an attacking army to meet the oncoming blaze Lasher's men had set. It would gobble up all fuel in its path as it charged; when the two fires met, they'd die.

If the east wind that blew Lasher's fire didn't rise . . . If Lasher's fire didn't crown . . .

More than once, wielding ax and saw and shovel like the rest, Fargo straightened, panting, looked toward the east. There, now, an immense pall of smoke hung low over the rim of the forest, a pale, gigantic cloud. But not as yet had any orange flicker appeared on its underside; the fire was still walking, had not crowned, had not begun to fly. Nearby, somebody yelled, "Timberrrr!" Fargo looked up automatically, stepped clear of a giant fir that crashed to earth two dozen yards away, then swung his own ax again.

The sun dropped, turned red as blood through the climbing veil of smoke. Damn it, Fargo wondered, where were the men from the lumber camp? His shoulders ached, his arms were leaden; still he kept on working in a dull haze of fatigue. But they could not go on like this much longer, not without help and not without food and rest. He snapped an order; somebody built a fire on rocks beside the creek, began to cook meat and brew hot coffee. In shifts, the men ate and drank and rested briefly; but only briefly, for always that pall of smoke drew nearer. In an hour, maybe less, the fire would be upon them.

With a tin cup of double-strength black brew in his hand, Fargo studied that haze, so much closer now. Then suddenly, he tensed and cursed. Suddenly the bottom of that cloud flamed brightly, turned orange. At the same moment, he was aware of a change and shift in wind.

Out there, miles away, the fire had crowned. Now it would come through the treetops at express-train speed.

They'd run out of time; if he were to set a backfire, it was now or never.

He threw down the cup and gave his orders. Men fanned out along the river and the clearing they had made. They thrust lighted torches into the needles on the ground, watched blazes spring to life under the blast of the rising wind. They spread quickly. Wildfire. The flickering orange tongue blew back toward the approaching crown fire. Smoke and sparks swirled upward.

Fargo lit a cigarette. All right. This was showdown. If the backfire worked, if it could eat alive all the fuel between here and Lasher's fire, if the wind held . . . He watched the flames grow, rush onward. It was going to be a battle of the giants . . .

Now the animals began to come. Fleeing ahead of Lasher's fire, they dashed through the flames that Fargo had set. Some of them made it; others, he knew, would be trapped and burned alive. Blacktail deer, elk, black bear, rabbits, squirrels, even a pair of moose — the presence of which he'd not suspected in the Wolf's Head — dashed through the smoke, plunged into Snow Fork, oblivious to the humans all around. With them loped the predators; he caught a glimpse of tan cougars moving fluidly through the fir; bobcats, with eyes wide and lambent, scuttled down the river bank. Once, he saw two full-grown wolves, followed by pups not quite yearling, fade through the timber. Wolves mated for life; this was a family fleeing together.

Some of the animals, when they came through, were on fire, fur flickering with bright, orange flames. One black bear almost made the river, then bawled horribly, fell, snapping and clawing at its own flaming body, not forty yards from Fargo. He watched it for a split second, then drew his Colt and fired. It twitched once and, mercifully, died. Fargo's face was grim. Men could die like that in forest fires, too.

The wind rose. Fargo clamped his

hat on tighter, smiling thinly. This was to his advantage, this change and increase in intensity. It would drive his fire more strongly against Lasher's, it would win the battle for him . . . He had saved the Wolf's Head . . . Now the wind increased to almost gale intensity . . . Then Davis, coming up to get a cup of coffee, stared across the river and let out a curse.

"Fargo!"

Fargo whirled. Mutely, Davis pointed.

Fargo stared, blinking.

It was impossible; it was absolutely impossible. That was the direction from which help should come — not another fire!

But there it was. Roaring toward them from a mile away. Along a narrow front but spreading rapidly, already crowned. Rushing through the treetops like charging cavalry, leaping from tree to tree, turning the tops of ancient firs to fiery orange bombs. It hurtled toward them with incredible speed. And they were trapped. Men and mules alike, they were caught between two fires.

Fargo stood poised for one frozen second. Then he bellowed at Davis, "The mules!" He plunged into the narrow stream with Davis right behind. He heard men yelling as they saw the flames, realized their predicament. Within minutes the fire would be upon them and there was one hope and only one. The stream rushed around Fargo's thigh's as he made the crossing, climbed the farther bank. Then he was among the tethered mules, slashing ropes with his Batangas knife; Davis, with his long-bladed Case was doing likewise.

Horses would have run into the flames; mules were different, smarter. As each broke free, it thunderd toward the stream. Now the flames were closer, not a quarter of a mile away. Fargo could feel the terrible heat that roiled ahead of a crown fire. It seemed to suck all oxygen from the air. The last minute, unleashed pounded past him.

He whirled on Davis. "The river!" he screamed.

The animals that had crossed it, bear and deer and cougars, came charging back. Fargo and Davis ran for water with them, ahead of a blast that charred the shirt on Fargo's back. When they reached the bank they plunged in. The rest of Fargo's men had already done the same. The water came, here in this pool, to Fargo's chest. He stood there for an instant, looking toward the oncoming crown fire. Now it was only yards away. It rushed with such force that it would leap the stream, devour all the timber they had cut, and, if they did not get beneath the water . . .

Fargo sucked in a breath of super-heated air. Then he dived.

Beneath the surface, he bumped something; to his surprise it was a bull elk. Like himself, it submerged its head; he actually clung to its antler for anchorage. It did not seem to mind, seemed oblivious to him. Water swirled around him; the scene below here was dreamlike, the faces of men, the heads of animals, all, for this instant, made one by this common danger.

A half minute passed, and it seemed a century. Fargo felt the pressure building in his lungs. The gasp of air he'd taken, oxygen already burned out of it, had been insufficient. He needed more; his chest ached, his temples throbbed. But he dared not rear above the surface of the water.

Overhead now, there would be a fire storm. He could feel the water, usually icy cold with melting snow, heating around him. God help the man who tried to break the surface and breathe now; he'd die with seared lungs.

That was what happened to the elk. It convulsed, kicked upward, raised its muzzle above the surface. Then it began to thresh. Fargo, his own chest bursting, vision blurred, reeled clear of the threshing hooves. Then the elk died, settling to the bottom slowly, in an obscene, slow motion ballet.

He closed his eyes, gritted teeth.

His chest was near exploding. The water grew hot around him; he thrust a hand above the surface, pulled it back, its skin already blistered. Christ! he thought. Burn or drown —

Then he could stand it no longer. Two minutes had passed, more; he had to have air. He shielded nose with hand, broke the surface in heat that was almost unbearable. It seared his throat and lungs, but it did not kill him. He got enough air to hold him for another minute, got a glimpse, too, of bright flame leaping across the river. He sank back.

An eternity passed. Then, chest throbbing, he had to rise again. He came up into a backwash of heat. The fire had leaped the river, ignited all the trees they had cut, raced through them. Now it was beginning to falter where the backfire had already burned.

Fargo pushed up through the steaming surface of the river. It was littered with corpses; mostly, they were animals. But something bumped against him

211

that was no animal; he looked. It was Davis, dead face contorted in the agony of having drawn in a chestful of super-heated air that had burned him alive inside.

Fargo retched into the river. Then he clambered out on the smouldering west bank — the bank from which help should have come. And from which, instead, had come the blaze that, with a bit more luck, would have trapped and burned them all.

The west bank was a shambles. Even as he watched, a great fir, now a charred hulk, gave up the ghost, crashed to earth in a shower of sparks. It was a black wasteland. Fargo's mouth thinned, and he winced as blistered lips ground together.

He knew now, looking at that charred desert. It all fitted together. Oh, God, yes, he knew; and, automatically, his hand went to the shotgun, water-soaked, but still locked around his chest with its sling.

Then he turned, looked eastward.

The fires had met, all of them. Orange light flickered on the vast cloud of smoke. Then it faded. They had eaten up all the fuel and now the changing wind pushed them back against the barrenness their flames had made, crowded them off from progress toward the south, shoved them up against the barrier of the Wolf's Head to the north. This fire could be contained now. If they went on working long and hard, if reinforcements came . . .

* * *

They came. Twenty-four men from the lumber camp, with MacKenzie and Duke Hotchkiss in the lead and wagons loaded with drag-pans, barrels of water, pressure pumps, and hose and all the fire-fighting equipment kept around a logging camp. MacKenzie's face was sooty, blistered, his eyebrows and lashes burned away. But when he saw Fargo, his mouth twisted in a grin of surprise and pleasure. "Thank God," he whispered, seizing Fargo's hand. "You're still alive."

"Jesus, Fargo," Duke thundered. "I don't see how you did it!" He shaded eyes with a huge hand, stared eastward. "That fire's almost out right now."

"Yes," Fargo said. "We thought you'd be here in a hurry. Instead, a crown fire came ahead of you. It damned near parboiled us all. It did kill some."

MacKenzie shook his head. "I can't understand it. We saw the smoke; then the messenger came. Every man in camp saddled up and we hit out hell-for-leather here. Then, not ten miles away we ran into fire on our side of the Fork. It had already crowned. The wind took it toward you. My heart stopped, thinking of all of you trapped in between. We had to hold back, come behind the fire . . ."

"Sure," said Fargo.

"Duke almost went crazy. He was ahead of us all the way, he was

so upset. Like a madman . . . "
MacKenzie rubbed his face. "Well,
a lot of Wolf's Head's gone. But
not so much that my lease will be
cancelled. If we can pinch this quadrant
out . . . "

"You can do it," Fargo said. "The
wind's with us. Of course, the winds
wouldn't have made any difference if
Lasher's men had been able to rub
us out like they tried to. Then the
fire could have burned on unchecked,
eaten up more than a quarter of the
Wolf's Head . . . "

Suddenly very tired, he sat down on a
rock. It was hot, almost incandescently
so, and he stood up again.

MacKenzie stared at him with
concern. "Fargo," he said, "you're
dead tired. You and your men take a
rest. We'll take care of the fire . . . "

"No, we'll help you, those of us that
are left."

"MacKenzie's right. Rest," Duke
said. "Judas Priest, Fargo, you look
like a drowned rat. How long were you

under water? I'll bet all your ammo's soaked."

"It is," said Fargo. "All right. We'll rest. You and the others go ahead."

"We'll do that," said MacKenzie, and he made a signal to move out. His cavalcade moved on into the burned land, with Duke riding beside him on a mule.

10

FARGO and his men, what was left of them, sat on the riverbank for an hour, all of them blistered and seared. Davis was not the only victim of the fire; in too shallow a pool, a man named Whipple had been cooked alive like a lobster when the water boiled around him. The rest of the survivors drank coffee and ate canned rations in stunned silence.

Finally Fargo stood up. "You men," he said, "gather what mules are left and head back to camp. You've all earned your pay and I'll see that each of you gets a bonus — the head price promised for Lasher's men. Christ knows, you've killed your share."

One of them, a hulking giant named Trelawny, stared at Fargo. "Ain't you goin' with us?"

217

"No," said Fargo, "I'm goin' to join the fire-crew."

Trelawny stood up. "Then we'll ride with you." He looked around. "Right? By God, we put our hands to this and we'll not turn loose until the fire's out."

Fargo smiled. Touched in spite of himself, he shook his head. "No. Head back for camp. There's no more danger of fire. Get some rest, I'll join you there after a while."

There was grumbling, but reluctantly, they departed. Fargo, with one saddle mule, was left alone in the smoking wilderness.

When they were out of sight he arose wearily. He opened the shotgun, jacked out the shells crammed in two more from his bandolier. He pointed the muzzles at the water, pulled the trigger. Nothing except the two dry clicks of firing pins.

His mouth twisted. He tried two more shells. As water-logged as the first, they failed too. The next pair of rounds yielded better results. One of them went off, but not with full thunder. Fargo judged the splatter they made on the surface. The water had got to the powder of that round, too.

He checked the bandolier. There were only three more rounds left in it. Probably they were as ineffectual as all the rest. He slung the shotgun. Then he tried the Colt.

The ammunition of that day was far from waterproof. The Colt failed thrice out of six rounds. Fargo nodded and sheathed the gun.

His Winchester had been left back on the slope where the battle had taken place. Later, he would retrieve it. For now, though, he could not depend on his guns.

That was all right. He knew what he could depend on.

He mounted the mule. Then he rode westward, toward the burn.

★ ★ ★

"Fargo!" MacKenzie looked at him out of eyes bloodshot with smoke. "Damn it, you ought to be back in camp."

"I'll go there when I'm sure the fire's out." Fargo's eyes went to the double-bitted ax MacKenzie held. The lumberman had been working alongside his crew, stroke for stroke in the charred wilderness, clearing fire lanes.

Fargo reached out, took the ax from MacKenzie's hand. "I want this," he said. "Where's the Duke?"

MacKenzie blinked. He gestured vaguely, south. "I don't know. Out there somewhere."

"I'll find him," Fargo said, and before MacKenzie could protest, vanished into the burn, moving carefully between smouldering firs which still dripped flaming branches.

He wound his way through the ruined forest, around charred trunks, stepping over the black-burnt bodies of game burned alive. He found working parties, inquired for Duke. They saw nothing wrong with that, directed him down the line. Fargo moved on, ax cradled in his palm, lips thin, boots making black puffs of charcoal as he walked.

Where the crown fire had passed it was like being on the moon. That desolate, that ruined. His gray eyes searched the barren reaches of what had once been lush wilderness, where everything was now black. Then he saw the Duke, hacking away with a double-bitted ax like Fargo's own, to bring down a spark-laden stump.

Fargo stopped. "Duke," he said.

Hotchkiss broke the ax's swing. He turned, his right hand wrapped around the handle. "Fargo. I thought you'd headed for camp."

"Not yet," Fargo said. "You and I have got things to talk about first."

Duke's big, square-jawed face split in a grin. "Like what?"

"Like, how much did Lasher pay you?"

Duke stared at him. Then his eyes lit and his grin widened. "You figured it all out, huh?"

"I figured it," said Fargo. "In Seattle you told me you had a full ticket. I had to fight you to sign on. But you signed Goodis."

"Right," said Duke, leaning easily on the grounded ax.

"Next, it was the Hoskins thing. Barbara played with his rope, sure, but you were the one that passed it to him around the trunk. She didn't cut it. You were the one that palmed the razor blade, made the slash before Hoskins went up the spar tree."

Duke's grin did not diminish by one iota. "You think that, huh?"

"I know it," Fargo said. "The clincher was when you sank that ax in Mannix — Morse, whoever — before he could talk. He knocked over that lamp figuring you would protect him. Instead, you killed him."

"You're smart, ain't you," Duke said.

"Smart enough to have started wondering after that. Then, today. You rode out with MacKenzie. Moved

222

ahead, he said so. And set the fire that crowned and trapped us. That was tricky . . . "

Duke laughed softly, not at all abashed. "Flamin' arrows. The Injuns used to use 'em. As soon as I was out of sight of MacKenzie, I set the trees on fire, up high."

"Yes," said Fargo. "You're Lasher's man."

"Right. He pays good. Damn good, more than a woods boss can make in a hell of a lot of seasons." Duke's heavy brows drew down. "I've worked for somebody else all my life, Fargo. I'll come out of this with enough to set up for myself."

Fargo said quietly, "You ain't comin' out of it."

Duke smiled faintly, "My skirts are clean. Nobody's got evidence against me. Except you." Then he raised the ax. "And you ain't gonna be in no condition to talk. This burn-out didn't work because of your patrols, but there'll be others. After you're dead."

Quickly, deftly, Fargo shifted his grip on his own ax. "Never cook your rabbit 'til you kill it."

"Hell, man, you're already dead. I cut my teeth on a double-bit." Then, with terrible force, Duke swung the ax.

The two-edged head was a blur in the sunlight as it ripped toward Fargo. He ducked, felt it riffle his hair as it whistled past. Then he was up, caught the backswing with his own blade. Steel rang against steel with a force Fargo felt all through his body. The backstroke knocked his blade down, and he shortened his grip as Duke recovered, came at him again, chopping now, to split Fargo's head.

Fargo caught Duke's ax on the top of his own blade. Again that chiming of steel. But Fargo had been fighting men and fire for hours; the force of Duke's blow drove the ax-handle down through his palms. Before he could get a fresh grip, Duke chopped once more.

The stroke would have split Fargo clean, from head to crotch, if it had landed. He turned his hands just in time, caught the blow on the length of handle protruding from beneath clenched hands. The blade sheared eight inches of the haft cleanly, but the impact deflected it just enough to miss Fargo.

Duke jumped back, laughing, confident. "Now you got a short ax — and I already had the reach on you. Git ready, Fargo, this is it." He edged forward like a boxer, balancing on the balls of his feet, weapon gripped by the very end of its handle. There was no way Fargo could get inside that swing, and he backed off and Duke came after him, pushing him, menacing him, waiting for the perfect moment, meanwhile savoring the advantage he had, the certainty it made him feel.

"Ha! Ha!, Fargo!" He swung forward, then backward, then forward; the ax, blade parallel to the ground like a giant pendulum at the end of his long arms.

It glittered, whistled, seeking Fargo's guts as he backed across the burn and Duke advanced. Fargo managed each time to stay just outside the arc of swing but that was because Duke was playing with him.

Then Duke's face changed, eyes suddenly lambent. "Now!" he roared as he moved in fast and this time chopped straight at Fargo's belly as if it were a tree trunk. The blade whistled at him from the left, and his own ax was in his right hand. It must have seemed to Duke there was no way he could fend the blow.

That was what Fargo had waited for. He flipped his right, caught the ax-handle with his left hand which was just as strong and deft, and caught Duke's mighty, finishing blow in mid-swing. Steel rang against steel with a loud, clear clang, and the force of Duke's blow which would have driven the blade all the way to the handle in wood, much less flesh, nearly knocked Fargo's weapon from his grasp and it spun him half around.

But the quick, unexpected block threw Duke even farther off balance. He had put everything he had into that swing; for an instant, as his blade sheered off of Fargo's toward the ground, he staggered. Fargo, recovering like a cat, whirled, used that desperate advantage. For it was now or never, and he came in over Duke's rising blade and swung his own, aiming high, putting every ounce of strength behind the blow.

He felt the ax-handle shudder in his hand. There was a sound almost exactly as if he had struck a tree trunk. Then the ax was free, moving on, finishing its swing.

Duke stepped back; his hand raised his weapon, his body poised, balanced on the balls of his feet.

Even headless, it seemed that he would continue to fight.

Then, spouting red, what was left of Duke fell forward, landed hard, kicked a half dozen times like a chicken with a wrung neck, lay still.

Fargo looked at the thing that had rolled from Duke's shoulders, and now, ten feet away on the burned ground, stared at him with sightless eyes.

He sucked in a long breath, dropped his ax.

Then, massively, he vomited.

This part of it, anyhow, was over.

He was still sitting there, too weak from reaction and the day's fighting to move, when MacKenzie came running to him.

11

ALEC MACKENZIE himself took over as woods boss when the last spark had been extinguished, and Fargo put his men back out on patrol.

Weeks passed. Driving his men furiously, MacKenzie got the timber out. There were no more accidents, no more fires, no sign of anyone strange roaming the Wolf's Head. The pond behind the dam filled with logs, and then it began to rain. At first the rains were small, insignificant, only a constant drizzle, and the men went on working. Then they set in full force, and the Wolf's Head began to fill. Water rushed over the dam; the logs strained at their booms like horses eager for a race.

There was no more danger of fire.

Fargo brought in his men. He and MacKenzie sat over good bourbon in the camp office, savoring an interval of rest, making plans.

"I think Lasher must have shot his bolt," the Scot said. "He's finished and he knows it."

"Maybe." Fargo appraised the amber glass with an expert's eye, then sipped. "Maybe not. We've still got to make the drive. I know Saul Lasher of old. You can't count him out until he's dead."

"Aye, he's a tough bastard. All the same, once we're in the river — "

"We'll have to be twice as careful," Fargo drank again. "You know what I'd do if I were Lasher? If I had mill contracts bearing down on me and no timber to fill 'em with?"

"What?"

"Take yours," said Fargo. "Hijack your drive."

"Hijack my drive?"

"Right. I'd get me some men, set up an ambush somewhere along the

Wolf's Head before it gets anywhere near civilization, figure out a way to jam the drive, and hit your outfit with everything I could scrape together. Wipe out all your men, take over with my own. Finish the drive down to the Sound, hide the logs in a cover somewhere, cut off your brand on their ends and put my own on, and sell 'em to a mill — there are plenty of pirate mills that don't ask questions. Take the money and get out of the country, let the other mills go to hell with their legitimate contracts and the banks foreclose." Fargo finished his drink. "A man like Lasher, with a hundred thousand or so of timber money from your wood could set himself up real nice in the mahogany *monterias* down in the Mexican jungle or along the Amazon."

"That would be an incredibly desperate act." MacKenzie shook his head.

"Lasher's a desperate man."

The Scot considered for a moment. "Then it'll be up to you again, Fargo.

To stick with us, make sure the drive goes through."

Fargo nodded. Absently, his hand caressed the double-barreled shotgun within close reach on the table. "That," he said, "is what I hired out for."

★ ★ ★

Three days later, at first light, they blew the Wolf's Head dam.

Fargo, caulks dug into a massive fir log, poised his peavey. When the dull thunder sounded far ahead the wood beneath his feet trembled like something suddenly come to life. Then, slowly, it floated forward, beginning the long journey down the Wolf's Head to Puget Sound. Minute by minute it picked up speed, and so did the tons of timber around, behind it. It bobbed, rolled in the freshening current of the rain-swollen stream, and then it rushed forward like a wild thing suddenly uncaged. Grinding and groaning, thousands more like it surged

232

along behind. They shot over the chute of the dam, slammed into the swirling water below, and hurtled down the flooded river to the coast.

As the banks sped by, Fargo's knees bent, caulks dug, feet deftly birling, balancing like a cat, felt a rush of exhilaration. It was good to be on the river again, riding the big wood hell-for-leather in white water; spray drenched him icily but he hardly felt it. There would not be many more drives like this; he was going to enjoy it while he could.

And he had, he thought, better damned well keep his balance. Logger's clothes were heavy enough if you went in. Laden with bandoliers, with slung shotgun and rifle as he was, he'd sink like a stone if he lost his balance.

If, he thought grimly, those millions of pounds of fir logs rushing along behind him didn't grind him to a bloody pulp first.

That was part of the game; that was where the fun came in, at least for him. The risk was what he lived for. He turned, looked back at his men behind him, busy with peaveys and cant-hooks. They too were armed; every man had a Winchester slung across his shoulders. If Lasher tried to stop the drive, he'd damned well better be prepared for war.

On downriver they surged, the wanigan full of bedrolls and cooking gear behind them. Sometimes they hit whirlpools and savage eddies from the suction of which the fir sticks must be wrenched with brute force and at incredible danger. Then white water, where hidden rocks like fangs sought to seize the logs and jam the drive. Once that happened; the great raft of floating fir piled up behind caught timbers in a huge, grinding dangerous mass. Then men worked furiously to free the jam but, in the end, it took dynamite. Then, released, the logs rushed on; the drive continued.

Three, four days of never-ending spray, of sleeping in wet blankets, of fighting water, rocks, and jamming logs. Then, ahead, the forest-clad hills gave way to cliffs, the river narrowed, foaming through a gorge. The logs rushed on at breakneck speed and Fargo braced himself. This was called the chute. There would be one hell of a wild ride through here where the river dropped swiftly between those sheer, towering cliffs. But it was not the way the logs picked up speed as they rushed into the narrow, rain-swollen channel like stampeding horses that made his heart beat faster. It was the realization that if Lasher were going to ambush the drive, this was the place.

Now cliffs towered over them, blocking out daylight; rain mixed with spray drenched them; the great drive pounded along at almost express-train speed. Fargo balanced like a cat, riding his rolling, bobbing, bucking stick of timber instinctively. Then he tensed. Up ahead, a quarter of a mile away, the chute turned sharply. What lay beyond the turn could not be guessed, but he managed to unsling the shotgun, even as the drive raced toward it.

Then, with Fargo at the front, MacKenzie nearby, the logs rushed around the turn. For a moment, the full force of rain and spray filled Fargo's eyes, blinding him. He shook his head, blinked, and then he saw it and he cursed, knowing his instinct had served him well. Up ahead the chute narrowed even more — and there great charges of dynamite had spilled tons of rock and earth into the river to block it.

MacKenzie let out a yell that the wind whipped away. Fargo motioned wildly, and he and MacKenzie ran back along the drive toward the rear, leaping nimbly from log to log. When the timber hit that barrier with the force at which it traveled, the front of the drive was no place to be. "Back!" Fargo screamed at his men. "Back! We're gonna jam!"

They barely made it. Up ahead there was a sound like a hundred train wrecks as enormous logs slammed full-tilt into the massive barrier. They reared and seemed to paw the air, then hung, jammed; and, rushing along behind them, the rest of the drive slammed into them and piled up, logs grinding, climbing, bucking, rolling, smashing together, tilting, or being shoved beneath the surface.

Beneath Fargo the whole world seemed to shudder, buck, and quake. Fighting to keep his balance as one end of the stick on which he stood was rammed deep under, he looked up just in time to see another log, five feet through the butt, override it, tower high above him, come crashing down. Fargo jumped sideways, his caulks caught in the wood of a stick of timber four, five feet away, and then he jumped again, and the rearing log crashed down exactly where he'd been seconds before. Then it drove forward like a battering ram, grating against the one beneath it.

And still it was a nightmare of thrusting, rearing, grinding wood. Fargo saw one of the river-hogs, a man named Curtis, fighting to keep his balance on a tilting log. Then, behind him, another stick came sliding forward, pushed by all those behind it. Fargo yelled, but his voice was lost in the sound of grinding, crashing wood, the swirl of rushing water, the wind and rain. The oncoming log hit Curtis like a mighty fist, knocked him forward. He fell into the water in a gap of three, four feet between two huge timbers. Fargo caught a glimpse of a white face, an upthrust hand. Slowly, brutally, like millstones, the jam's force ground the great logs together. The man's scream was high, thin, and pinched off quickly.

Then the logs shuddered to a final halt beneath the feet of the rivermen as the jam stabilized. The whole channel of the river was a solid floor of logs from wall to wall, blocked by the barrier, extending nearly a mile upstream.

And then, as MacKenzie's loggers steadied themselves, got their footing once again, they came — Lasher's men.

There was a cleft in the gorge wall up by the barrier. Out of that they poured, three dozen of them, and they came shooting. Like ants they swarmed out on the vast jam and Fargo, taking cover behind a tilted log, grinned coldly as he recognized the big man in the lead, dressed in logger's clothes and with a Colt Peacemaker in each hand.

So this was it, the final fight. Fargo yelled, "Here they come! Give 'em hell!" His own men fanned out, sheltering. Lasher's men spread across the jam, took shelter, too. Fargo saw Lasher fall behind a log, snap a shot around its end. He lined his Winchester, took aim, but Lasher drew back just as Fargo's bullet plowed splinters.

Now the canyon was thunderous with echoing gunfire, as MacKenzie's men returned Lasher's fire. Lead whipped like sleet across the jam, whined and ricocheted off the canyon walls. Then there was more firing from above. Lasher had men on the gorge rims, too, and they could shoot down on the jam, pick off the loggers like fish in a barrel!

Fargo rolled, found better shelter as a bullet chopped wood by his face. That meant they were outnumbered and under attack from three sides, and Lasher had them unless somebody did something quick — and he would have to be the one. He twisted, looked over his shoulder to the rear of the drive. It was a long way back to the wanigan, the big scow that held the bedrolls and supplies and followed the drive down river. Right now it was piled up at the rear of the jam a mile away.

That was, Fargo thought, a long way to have to go for dynamite.

But he had to have it; there was no other way.

He turned, began to work his way toward the rear. He slithered in and out between the piled, awry logs like a snake. Bullets plunked around him but his use of cover was adept; no one up on the rim or out on the jam had a fair shot at him.

He found MacKenzie crouched behind a timber levering shot after shot from a Winchester. The Scot looked startled as Fargo crawled up alongside. Fargo tapped him on the arm. "Keep me covered, I'm going after dynamite!"

"Dynamite? Man, ye'll never make it through all this with dynamite!"

"I'll make it! Tell the men to rake those rims, make those birds up there keep their heads down. They do that, I've got a chance!" Then he crawled on.

Behind him he heard Lasher's voice ring out. "MacKenzie! You'll save a lot of lives if you surrender! I've got you whipsawed! You haven't got a chance!"

"Go to hell!" the Scot shouted back. "Ye wouldn't leave a man alive to tell the tale of this, ye bastard!" And the Scot's rifle roared.

Grinning tightly, Fargo scuttled along

the jam. All around him huge logs were heaped like giant matchsticks tossed together. Even so, lead bit dangerously close, and now he was reaching the worst part. Back here at the drive's rear the jam was not so bad — which meant that the cover thinned. Hunkering behind a log Fargo could see the wanigan forced against the jam by the current a hundred yards away. A hundred yards of open space he'd have to cross, leaping from log to log, under fire. And then cross once more, the other way — carrying dynamite.

All right. That was what MacKenzie paid him for. He slung the shotgun, unlimbered the Winchester. His eyes raked the gorge rims right and left. He caught a flicker of movement. He aimed carefully, fired.

Up there a man screamed, rose to full height, came toppling down the canyon wall, landed on the jam, sprawled like a rag doll. Fargo's eye went quickly to the other rim. A head appeared, trying to see what had happened. Fargo snapped another shot; it vanished. Then, giving the gunmen on the wall that to think about, he leaped to his feet and ran across the open space, spiked boots driving. As he ran he levered the Winchester mechanically, snapping shot after shot at the rims above. Lead whipped about him, chunked into the logs. He had almost made the wanigan when he was knocked sideways by a terrific impact.

He lay there, stunned for a second. Then, feeling no pain or shock at all, he realized what had happened. A slug had plowed into the rifle stock, slammed it against his belly. The gun was ruined, but now he was only feet from the big scow.

The cook and bullcook who poled it had taken cover on the jam. Fargo rolled into the boat, scrambled toward its center where, carefully stowed among the bedrolls were boxes of dynamite, caps, and fuses, covered with tarpaulins to keep them dry. They were for blowing jams like this one.

Sprawled behind the shelter of the gunwales, he got a box open, raked out sticks of dynamite already clipped together in bundles of three and four and five. He found a bedroll, slit its lashings with the Batangas knife, crammed in a half dozen bombs of dynamite, lashed it shut. Then he opened another one, loaded it with caps and fuse, rolled it tight, rolled yet another bedroll around it. The dynamite was fresh; if hit by a bullet it probably wouldn't go. But if the caps took a hit they packed enough power to blow him to kingdom come all by themselves.

Fargo took a long breath, braced himself. Then, with a bundle of blanket-wrapped explosive under either arm, he came out of the wanigan in a great bound and lit running, darting across the open like a frightened rabbit.

From up on the rims bullets chopped around him. Then his heart seemed to stop as something slammed into the bundle of dynamite, nearly tearing it form his hand. A rifle slug! But it had missed the powder, only chipping the blankets. Ahead, he saw an upthrust log — cover, shelter. He dived awkwardly, trying to protect dynamite and caps alike from impact.

He made it. Now at least he had a chance. He lay there panting, then scrambled to his feet. Dodging, weaving, crawling, he ran forward across the jam, taking advantage of every bit of cover. Rifle fire had swelled to a crescendo now.

Nearly a half mile, over a devil's tangle of jammed fir, under and around big logs, with lead ripping all about him and enough explosives in his arms to make him vanish without trace if someone scored a lucky hit. It was the longest, most endless distance he had ever covered. Then, ahead, he saw MacKenzie, still behind his log, still shooting with machine-like regularity. Fargo leaped, landed behind him.

The Scot whirled; then his eyes

widened as he recognized Fargo and saw the bundles. "Ye got it?"

"I got it," Fargo said. He grinned. Well-sheltered now, he slit the lashings with the Filipino knife.

MacKenzie laughed happily. "Here, lemme help." He seized dynamite, caps, fuses. He and Fargo crimped in the caps, inserted fuses. Within two minutes their bombs were armed. MacKenzie took out a waterproof match case.

He handed Fargo half the matches. Then, grinning, he said harshly, "Let's git 'em, Fargo!"

"Right!" Fargo said.

He and MacKenzie leaped up, ran forward, Lasher and his men saw them coming, concentrated a hail of fire upon them. But they had cover; most of the bullets plowed into the logs. Then MacKenzie stumbled. "Fargo," he yelled and fell, pitching the two dynamite bombs he carried as he went down with a bullet in his thigh.

Fargo scooped them out of mid-air

with a desperate lurch, hugged them to his chest. "Go on!" MacKenzie shouted. Fargo ducked beneath a log, rolled across the jam holding the dynamite clear, came up behind another huge stick of fir that was like the parapet of a trench with the excellent shelter it provided. He crouched low, struck a match, held it to the fuse. Then he heard what he was listening for — a hiss. Fargo threw the dynamite, lobbing it toward the head of the jam without rising above his cover.

He could see the bomb sailing lazily through the air, trailing a fine thread of smoke. He watched it drop out of sight somewhere up near the barrier, and lit another one. Suddenly the whole gorge seemed to convulse with the confined thunder of the explosion. Men screamed. Fargo threw another bomb, and another.

They went off up there, and all sorts of things flew into the air — wood and bits of metal that had once been guns, and other things, ragged, bloody. Fargo swarmed up from behind his log and ran forward into swirling smoke that reeked of powder and of death. He had two more bombs left, and he lit one as he went, then hurled it straight for the barrier.

He dropped, and when the five sticks went off, threw the other one. He was about to jump up again, charge on into smoke with his shotgun, when a strange thing happened.

Beneath him, the jam gave a mighty shudder and groaned like a giant in agony. Logs began to move, slightly but definitely. There was a grinding sound. Fargo swore, half in amazement, half in delight.

It was as close to a miracle as he could ask for. Normally such a jam could be broken only by charges carefully placed beneath key logs by experts. But behind the jam the rushing river had been rising, piling up. Beneath the jam it must have been eating at, undercutting, the barrier. And the force of those explosions had breached the dam, let that rushing torrent through and shaken loose the logs up there, and now as the torrent rolled boulders aside as if they were pebbles, swept the rubble down the stream, the drive was free and moving.

After that it was a nightmare, and there was no time for the survivors either side to shoot. The breaking of the jam was as convulsive and as deadly as its forming had been. Huge logs rolled and tossed and splashed and ground, some went under, some bobbed up. Men screamed, especially Lasher's men, up there at the head, caught by surprise in the vast upheaval, the breaking free. Fargo dodged hurtling sticks of timber, fought to keep his balance, leaped from log to log as the jam broke and then went roaring down the river. He caught a glimpse of MacKenzie lying flat, clinging to a huge fir for dear life.

Then the log drive was a living, stampeding, rampaging thing again, rushing along. It spread out, rushed down the river. Fargo rode a giant stick of timber like a cat, shotgun unslung. His eyes searched the huge mass of rocketing fir.

Some of Lasher's men were left. They clung to the logs or rode them like true river-hogs, but they were in no mood for fighting; they were dazed, in shock. Fargo knew, though, that they'd recover. He aimed the shotgun. It roared once, twice, and three of Lasher's men went down. He broke the weapon, crammed in new rounds.

Then he thought he heard a yell of warning behind him. *"Fargo!"* He whirled on his bucking, lashing perch. MacKenzie, clinging to a log nearby, gestured. Then Fargo saw him — Lasher, running nimbly toward him across the drive, leaping from log to log, face contorted, a Colt in either hand. Fargo aimed the shotgun, pulled both triggers.

At exactly that instant his log slammed into another. The impact nearly threw him into the river. The double charge went wide, and Lasher kept on coming. He leaped a gap of swirling water and then, earing back the hammers of his Colts, he was on the end of Fargo's log.

"Damn you, Fargo!" he grated. "You've ruined me, but you'll not live to laugh about it!"

Just before Lasher pulled the triggers, Fargo shoved his caulks deep into the log, gave it a push with every ounce of strength in his muscular legs. Floating free, the big log revolved.

As it spun beneath his feet Fargo ran with it, birling, and he saw Lasher teeter, lose his balance. One of Lasher's Colts roared, but the shot went wild. Then Fargo had out his own .38 and he fired from the hip. The hollowpoint caught Lasher in the chest, picked him up and threw him backwards. He fell along the log, face white, eyes wide, amazed, as he died. Then he rolled into the water. Another log, hurtling at express-train speed, slammed into his body, ground it against the butt of the one on which Fargo stood. The two logs slammed together, bounced apart, and when they did, Lasher had vanished. It was over, finished. Only a sputtering of gunfire along the jam as MacKenzie's men cleaned up the rest of Lasher's crew persisted for a minute or two and then died away.

Fargo holstered the Colt, slung the shotgun. Then he leaped across the drive to the log where MacKenzie clung. He bent over the wounded man and helped him to his feet.

MacKenzie leaned against Fargo. "Nothin'," he said. "Jest my leg. Only a scratch, be all right when shock wears off." He raised his head, looked forward where the gorge was ending now, the river spreading out, swift, wild, free and open.

"Fargo," MacKenzie said with a quality of wonder in his voice. "Fargo, we're gonna make it."

"Yes," said Fargo.

Then they were in the clear, the logs

slowing and floating smoothly. "Yes, we're gonna make it." It seemed to him that he could already smell the sea.

He thought of The Colonel. He thought of twenty thousand dollars. And he thought of Lynne Houghton waiting in Seattle to help him spend it.

Then, walking carefully, he helped the wounded MacKenzie back along the drive to the wanigan.

THE END

FIGHTING RAMROD
Charles N. Heckelmann

Most men would have cut their losses, but Frazer counted the bullets in his guns and said he'd soak the range in blood before he'd give up another inch of what was his.

LONE GUN
Eric Allen

Smoke Blackbird had been away too long. The Lequires had seized the Blackbird farm, forcing the Indians and settlers off, and no one seemed willing to fight! He had to fight alone.

THE THIRD RIDER
Barry Cord

Mel Rawlins wasn't going to let anything stand in his way. His father was murdered, his two brothers gonc. Now Mel rode for vengeance.

ARIZONA DRIFTERS
W. C. Tuttle

When drifting Dutton and Lonnie Steelman decide to become partners they find that they have a common enemy in the formidable Thurston brothers.

TOMBSTONE
Matt Braun

Wells Fargo paid Luke Starbuck to outgun the silver-thieving stagecoach gang at Tombstone. Before long Luke can see the only thing bearing fruit in this eldorado will be the gallows tree.

HIGH BORDER RIDERS
Lee Floren

Buckshot McKee and Tortilla Joe cut the trail of a border tough who was running Mexican beef into Texas. They stopped the smuggler in his tracks.

BRETT RANDALL, GAMBLER
E. B. Mann

Larry Day had the choice of running away from the law or of assuming a dead man's place. No matter what he decided he was bound to end up dead.

THE GUNSHARP
William R. Cox

The Eggerleys weren't very smart. They trained their sights on Will Carney and Arizona's biggest blood bath began.

THE DEPUTY OF SAN RIANO
Lawrence A. Keating and Al. P. Nelson

When a man fell dead from his horse, Ed Grant was spotted riding away from the scene. The deputy sheriff rode out after him and came up against everything from gunfire to dynamite.

FARGO: MASSACRE RIVER
John Benteen

The ambushers up ahead had now blocked the road. Fargo's convoy was a jumble, a perfect target for the insurgents' weapons!

SUNDANCE: DEATH IN THE LAVA
John Benteen

The Modoc's captured the wagon train and its cargo of gold. But now the halfbreed they called Sundance was going after it . . .

HARSH RECKONING
Phil Ketchum

Five years of keeping himself alive in a brutal prison had made Brand tough and careless about who he gunned down . . .

FARGO: PANAMA GOLD
John Benteen

With foreign money behind him, Buckner was going to destroy the Panama Canal before it could be completed. Fargo's job was to stop Buckner.

FARGO:
THE SHARPSHOOTERS
John Benteen

The Canfield clan, thirty strong were raising hell in Texas. Fargo was tough enough to hold his own against the whole clan.

PISTOL LAW
Paul Evan Lehman

Lance Jones came back to Mustang for just one thing — revenge! Revenge on the people who had him thrown in jail.

HELL RIDERS
Steve Mensing

Wade Walker's kid brother, Duane, was locked up in the Silver City jail facing a rope at dawn. Wade was a ruthless outlaw, but he was smart, and he had vowed to have his brother out of jail before morning!

DESERT OF THE DAMNED
Nelson Nye

The law was after him for the murder of a marshal — a murder he didn't commit. Breen was after him for revenge — and Breen wouldn't stop at anything . . . blackmail, a frameup . . . or murder.

DAY OF THE COMANCHEROS
Steven C. Lawrence

Their very name struck terror into men's hearts — the Comancheros, a savage army of cutthroats who swept across Texas, leaving behind a bloodstained trail of robbery and murder.

SUNDANCE: SILENT ENEMY
John Benteen

A lone crazed Cheyenne was on a personal war path. They needed to pit one man against one crazed Indian. That man was Sundance.

LASSITER
Jack Slade

Lassiter wasn't the kind of man to listen to reason. Cross him once and he'll hold a grudge for years to come — if he let you live that long.

LAST STAGE TO GOMORRAH
Barry Cord

Jeff Carter, tough ex-riverboat gambler, now had himself a horse ranch that kept him free from gunfights and card games. Until Sturvesant of Wells Fargo showed up.

McALLISTER ON THE COMANCHE CROSSING
Matt Chisholm

The Comanche, McAllister owes them a life — and the trail is soaked with the blood of the men who had tried to outrun them before.

QUICK-TRIGGER COUNTRY
Clem Colt

Turkey Red hooked up with Curly Bill Graham's outlaw crew. But wholesale murder was out of Turk's line, so when range war flared he bucked the whole border gang alone . . .

CAMPAIGNING
Jim Miller

Ambushed on the Santa Fe trail, Sean Callahan is saved by two Indian strangers. But there'll be more lead and arrows flying before the band join Kit Carson against the Comanches.

GUNSLINGER'S RANGE
Jackson Cole

Three escaped convicts are out for revenge. They won't rest until they put a bullet through the head of the dirty snake who locked them behind bars.

RUSTLER'S TRAIL
Lee Floren

Jim Carlin knew he would have to stand up and fight because he had staked his claim right in the middle of Big Ike Outland's best grass.

THE TRUTH ABOUT SNAKE RIDGE
Marshall Grover

The troubleshooters came to San Cristobal to help the needy. For Larry and Stretch the turmoil began with a brawl and then an ambush.

WOLF DOG RANGE
Lee Floren

Will Ardery would stop at nothing, unless something stopped him first — like a bullet from Pete Manly's gun.

DEVIL'S DINERO
Marshall Grover

Plagued by remorse, a rich old reprobate hired the Texas Troubleshooters to deliver a fortune in greenbacks to each of his victims.

GUNS OF FURY
Ernest Haycox

Dane Starr, alias Dan Smith, wanted to close the door on his past and hang up his guns, but people wouldn't let him.

DONOVAN
Elmer Kelton

Donovan was supposed to be dead. Uncle Joe Vickers had fired off both barrels of a shotgun into the vicious outlaw's face as he was escaping from jail. Now Uncle Joe had been shot — in just the same way.

CODE OF THE GUN
Gordon D. Shirreffs

MacLean came riding home, with saddle tramp written all over him, but sewn in his shirt-lining was an Arizona Ranger's star.

GAMBLER'S GUN LUCK
Brett Austen

Gamblers seldom live long. Parker was a hell of a gambler. It was his life — or his death . . .

ORPHAN'S PREFERRED
Jim Miller

Sean Callahan answers the call of the Pony Express and fights Indians and outlaws to get the mail through.

DAY OF THE BUZZARD
T. V. Olsen

All Val Penmark cared about was getting the men who killed his wife.

THE MANHUNTER
Gordon D. Shirreffs

Lee Kershaw knew that every Rurale in the territory was on the lookout for him. But the offer of $5,000 in gold to find five small pieces of leather was too good to turn down.